I0557160

The Pleasures Collection
Book Two

SURRENDERED PLEASURES

a novel

by
Natasha Simmons

Surrendered Pleasures

Copyright © 2013 by Natasha D.T. Simmons

All rights reserved. The reproduction, transmission or utilization of this work in whole or in part in any form by any means, is forbidden.

This is a work of fiction. Names characters, places and incidents are purely fictional and products of the author's imagination. Any resemblances to actual persons, living or dead are entirely coincidental. Any references to actual places and businesses are used fictitiously.

ISBN-13: 978-0988299405
ISBN-10: 0988299402

Cover photography provided by: Michele Williamson

Author photo provided by: K.S. Photography

To Phil, with love.

ACKNOWLEDGEMENTS

Special thanks to all of you who read *Simple Pleasures* and wanted more. Thank you for waiting patiently for Candice and Landon's story and for allowing me to share it with you. You have no idea how much I appreciate your words of encouragement and support.

Thank you so much, Adrienne, Bobbie and Stacy for taking the time to read my manuscript.
Your input was invaluable.

…And to my Kori, your brilliant idea added a new dimension to the story. You are awesome!

"I surrender."

Prologue

Guidance

"Paulette Summers asked me today if we were expecting any grandkids anytime soon. Can you believe that, Dixon? I didn't realize people knew Joshua was even married. Grandkids? She couldn't possibly be serious."

From the chair next to his, Jocelyn Phoenix looked at her husband. Both she and Dixon took really great care of themselves, and to her, they didn't look like grandparents. She still had the same slim figure she had when they got married; unlike many of her friends, she didn't need any work done. Her fair skin was tight and flawless and besides the speckle of gray in his curly black hair, her husband had the body and looks of a much younger man—not a man in his sixties.

Not that she wasn't ready for her sons to start giving her grandchildren; Jocelyn Phoenix still was not pleased her son married a woman she didn't know anything about. She held out hope he would come to his senses soon and get back with Victoria, a more suitable mate for him.

Her husband Dixon did not speak. It was their designated recreational reading time. She stared at him. He never looked up from the fishing magazine—thumbing through it knowing it irritated the hell out of her.

Flipping through a fishing magazine did not fit the image Jocelyn tried to portray.

"Dixon did you hear me?"

"Yes."

"And? Don't you have anything to say to that?"

"I'm looking forward to grandkids." He didn't look up, just kept casually looking through the magazine.

"Well of course we need grandsons to continue on the legacy we've built, but *that girl* from Baton Rouge won't do. We don't know anyone from Baton Rouge. Joshua needs a wife who'll be strong enough to steer him away from that frivolous lifestyle he wants, not encourage him to sail most of the year like some pirate."

Jocelyn placed her hand on her chest. "She owns a bar for God's sake! And for that matter, it's also time for Landon to settle down."

She looked pointedly at her husband over the rim of her glasses.

"If we aren't careful we will end up with some little Euro-trash bastard from him." She waved her hand in the air and frowned in disgust. "Flying airplanes for a living won't have your name on a hospital wing. He needs to find a nice home here in Boston and settle down." Dixon looked up at his wife, but she continued. "He's never been serious about anyone and it's about time."

Dixon could take no more of her ranting and spoke. "I thought he and Candice, Alexandra's friend, got along well together. Landon seemed very taken with her." He saw the frown on his wife's face deepen, ignored it and continued. "From the brief meetings we've had, she seems like a fine woman and Joshua says she is quite talented. But who Landon chooses is none of our business." He looked pointedly at his wife. "None of our business Jocelyn."

"Surely you can't be serious Dixon. She's some no-name artist, and divorced at that!" She spat out the words as if the girl had leprosy.

Jocelyn leaned in towards Dixon and whispered, like she was afraid that just by saying the words out loud, other people would know, "Plus I overheard Joshua and Alex say her husband used to beat her. We don't want that kind of woman raising our grandsons."

Dixon could stand no more of his wife's nonsense. He tossed the magazine on the table beside the chair and stood to leave. "I'm going for a drive."

She looked down at the book she had in her lap. "It's nearly time to get ready for the fundraiser." Then looked up at him, "As head of the committee, I need to be there early to tend to the last minute details." Her voice was quiet and matter of fact. She returned to her book as if she was deity and there was nothing more to be said.

"I'm not going to the fundraiser."

"Of course you are." Not looking away from her book. She sat erect and still in their living room chair that could be described much like herself: elegant, formal, and stiff.

Though she was African-American, her face was very pale and nearly white. Looking up at him would make his revelation plausible, so she focused on the words in her book. To have her husband not accompany her to a function was unthinkable. They were always complemented on being a handsome powerful couple and tonight would be no different.

Just as everything in the living room had its place and every place held a purpose, she felt much the

9

same about everything and everyone, especially her family. They had their place in Boston's elite society and with that, came responsibility to maintain it.

Her sons were already running amuck, a situation that must be rectified, so when her husband Dixon Phoenix announced he was deviating from what she felt was his place, surely she must have heard him wrong.

She only had to shift her eyes to see him standing there, but refused to do so. She refused to look at him. Refused to see the look on his face. It was there more and more over the past six months. It left her angry and uneasy. Afraid. Fearful of the unknown shadow lurking around her, threatening to disrupt the control she had on her world, her husband.

"Why are you being so defiant Dixon?" She finally put her book down and faced him.

"I'm not a child, Jocelyn, I'm your husband. The sooner you understand that the better." Dixon turned to leave the room.

"Yes." The single word she spoke so simply, hung in the air a moment then fell heavily around the room. It halted his steps.

Dixon looked over his shoulder, narrowed his eyes and said, "You say that as if they are one in the same." Jocelyn placed her book on the end table, stood, smoothed the sides of her hair and adjusted the bun at the nape of her neck.

He turned completely to face her.

She pulled her glasses down slightly on the bridge of her nose, looked over the rim and said, "You have never complained about my guidance before."

Dixon squeezed his eyes shut, shook his head, and then stared at his wife as if seeing her for the first time.

"Guidance? Is that what you're calling what your total dictatorship of this family has been?"

She didn't waiver.

"Your 'guidance' has basically left our sons estranged to us. I told you when Joshua got married that enough was enough. You didn't approve of any of Joshua's decisions. Even before that you tried to exclude him from the family and pawn him off on my brother because his skin was darker than ours. What kind of mother does that to her child? I can't believe all the things I let you get away with in this family."

Dixon took a deep breath and shook his head as if mentally berating himself. "I'm just glad Josh and Landon never let you come between them. But, my dear Jocelyn, your reign is over."

"My guidance, Dixon, has made us one of the richest and most influential families in Boston. You

11

never complained when I orchestrated which events you should go to and who you should meet in order to close a deal. Do you think I chair fundraisers and host benefits just because I like to do it? I do it because it's what you need me to do. Just like it's obvious the boys need my direction in choosing the right women who will be beneficial to them."

Dixon walked over to the fireplace and rested a hand on the mantel as if he needed to put distance between he and his wife.

"Beneficial? What about women who will love them, care for them, and make them happy? Or are those concepts foreign to you?" He took a deep breath. "That's what they need. Joshua is already married to a lovely girl. And I'll tell you something else;

"I think you've said enough."

"Have I? Have I, Jocelyn?"

She smoothed the side of her hair again.

"Yes, you're getting yourself all worked up for no reason."

"Just as I thought; you haven't heard a word I've said." Dixon sighed as in defeat and looked directly at her. "I'm envious as hell of Joshua, because I never had a woman who made me smile just because she came into a room."

He waited for a glimmer of emotion.

12

Jocelyn ignored completely the insinuation that she never made him happy. "That won't last. He jumped into that marriage too quickly. Joshua was just upset with Victoria and me at the moment and married Alexandra to retaliate. I shouldn't have sent her to New Orleans to surprise him. I should have waited until he returned to Boston to show him that Victoria would be the perfect wife at his side. Her family has great connections. They could do great things in the business world together." She turned to pick up the book and glasses as if all words that needed to be spoken had been spoken. She looked at Dixon again and said, "I'm going to get dressed now. Your tuxedo is hanging in the closet of your dressing room."

"I told you I'm not going."

"That is not an option."

"Let me give you a few options, Jocelyn Phoenix. Option 1: You shut up and go to the fundraiser without me but, accompanied by my check. Option 2: You keep telling me what you think my options are and you get to go to the fundraiser without me or my check. And option 3, which is really not an option at all: If you do anything that interferes with Joshua and Alexandra's lives or Landon's life, I'm calling a lawyer and doing what I should have done years ago. The choice is yours." Dixon walked to the coat closet, grabbed his coat and walked towards the kitchen door that led to the garage.

Jocelyn called out after him, "Where are you going, Dixon Phoenix?"

"I'm going to hell; I need a vacation from you."

Chapter 1

Naked at the Door

He'd seen plenty of naked women, but never one quite like this. With his palms pressed flat against the door, Landon's eye nearly touched the glass of the peephole. He could feel the coolness of the metal that encased it, not believing the brazen woman who had the gall to stand on the other side of the hotel room door completely naked. Well, not completely naked, she had on his pilot hat.

Not used to turning down naked willing women, he opened the door, grabbed her wrist and pulled her inside before looking up and down the corridor for anyone who may be lurking at one o'clock in the morning. He turned to face her.

"Did you miss me?" She purred. He smiled and led her to the bedroom of his suite. He stopped at the foot of the bed, reached for the hat and tossed it on the chair. Landon smiled again, but the sparks that shot from his usual playful and sometimes a bit devious eyes, made them appear dark gray and dangerous.

"No need to ask why you are here Shelly," he said, never looking away from her face, "but what I do want to know is how did you know I was here?"

"I have a room down the hall. I saw you get off the elevator and walk to yours when I was headed to the workout area earlier. I figured I would just come prepared since you love to see me naked."

Shelly was a flight attendant he'd met more than two years ago. She had never worked on any of his flights but often when they were in New York at the same time they would meet in her hotel room to satisfy their sexual desires. Shelly was a great lover, had a gorgeous body and excited Landon in the bedroom to a degree, but other than that, she had nothing that could hold his attention.

She had begun to get clingy and expected him to see her when they were both in the same cities. So a month ago he ended whatever she thought was going on between them; apparently she had not gotten the message the first time or she would not have shown up at his door without knowing if he was alone or expecting someone. She certainly would now.

Shelly reached to begin unbuttoning Landon's shirt, but was stilled by the grip of his hand on her wrist. With his other hand he reached for the hotel robe

16

lying on the foot of his bed and shoved it towards her. She instinctively grabbed it.

"I'm sorry to tell you Sweetheart, but this is not going to happen." She stood there, eyes widening, then narrowing into slits. "What are you saying, Landon?"

"I am saying again, what I told you last month." She made no move to put on the robe. "I enjoyed the times we spent together, but I am in no way wanting now nor have I ever offered you a relationship." She rolled her eyes. "You knew what this was when we got involved. I made sure you did. I don't do relationships, I don't do long term anything, I don't do sleepovers, and I definitely don't do surprise visits, naked or otherwise."

"Oh but you have no problem doing *me*?" She snapped.

"If you were listening, you would have gotten the point that I especially do not do you, not anymore. Now if you don't mind, I have an early morning and would appreciate if you put the robe on and left." He walked to the door of the bedroom and indicated with a dramatic wave towards the hotel room door that that's the direction he intended for her to go in. She dropped the robe at her feet, passed so close to him he could smell the shampoo in her hair, and sauntered her naked behind out into the hotel hallway.

17

He was furious with her for showing up at his door unannounced but the gentleman in him could not let a naked woman walk away alone in public without making sure she arrived in her room unharmed. He also wondered how she would get in with no key.

Landon opened the door and watched as she removed her key from a plant in the hall, walked to her door, bent over slightly to slide the key in the slot and turned to look at him. His manhood stirred to life and he immediately questioned his sanity for sending her away, but his cell phone rang, startling him. Who would be calling at this hour, he thought. Shelly's eyes became slits again, seemingly assured the call was the reason he'd sent her away.

Landon didn't miss the look, nor did he care that she probably woke the entire floor when the door slammed shut.

He looked at his caller ID, smiled, then clicked to answer it.

"Hello Sweetie. Are you still the sexiest woman in New York?"

"Indeed I am. Hola, mi mejor amigo."

"You know you drive me crazy when you say it like that," he replied smiling as he walked to and stretched out on the sofa. The TV was on but he paid no attention to it.

18

"Save that crap for your women! Why didn't you call me when you got in town?"

"Who says I'm in town?" He loved toying with her.

"I say so, because if you weren't, you never would have had the balls to pick up the phone to tell me you weren't coming."

Sophia knew Landon better than anyone. Their relationship had started out as a casual fling, but had since turned into one of understanding, respect, and to both their surprise, a rich friendship. Landon could talk to Sophia about anything and even without the sex; they had a great time together. He couldn't wait to see her.

Landon laughed, knowing Sophia was exactly right about avoiding her call if he hadn't made it to town.

"So , when are you headed to Boston?"

Landon didn't want to tell Sophia about his side trip to Baton Rouge. She assumed he would be flying to see his family in Boston after their lunch tomorrow.

"I have a flight after lunch tomorrow." Landon got up and walked to the window. He looked out, but paid no attention to the many lights twinkling in the night.

19

His sister-in-law Alexandra commissioned him to fly to Baton Rouge to convince her best friend Candice to go on an extended trip to celebrate Candice's birthday.

Since Alex and Candice were so close, Candice had become part of the family and she and Landon spoke often, mostly when Candice couldn't reach her friend and his brother because they sailed so often.

He hadn't seen her in a while and wondered if she'd ever filed for divorce from the husband who was so abusive to her. She never brought up her husband when they talked and following her lead, he didn't either.

"You sound very vague. Are you keeping something from me?"

"I'm not sounding any kind of way. Look, it's late. I better get going."

"So who is she?" She asked deciding to change the subject.

"Who's who?"

"You know who, the warm body that is either on her way or who has just left."

Landon smiled, rubbed his hand over his head and gripped his neck as if trying to relieve tension. "Would you believe I just turned away a woman who showed up at my door naked?" Landon walked back to the door and looked through the peephole making sure talking about her hadn't conjured her up.

"Do tell," Sophia said.

Landon relayed the story of Shelly's arrival and departure. "Can you believe that, Soph?"

"No, I can't. What's gotten into you lately?" Sophia asked with a twinge of concern. "When do you ever turn women down?"

Landon explained to her that he meant he couldn't believe Shelly had shown up naked.

"I know what you meant." She paused again. "You haven't been quite the same since your brother Joshua got married. Is there a connection there? Is the great Landon Phoenix ready to settle down?"

"What do you mean by that?" He blurted out much quicker than he intended.

Other than the fact that he liked to be the one doing the chasing, he couldn't really understand why he'd recently preferred staying home most nights when he finally got the chance to be back in his own flat in London.

"Since you did not give your standard reply of 'Hell No!' I have only to gather that my assumption is in fact correct. I will see you tomorrow at the usual spot at the usual time. Te amo." She was gone before he had a chance to tell her how absurd she was.

Landon turned off the lamp near the sofa and clicked the remote to turn the TV off. The clock said 1:38 and he was exhausted. What a long day. He had taken time off from his job with British Airways and flew into New York as a passenger instead of the pilot this trip. He planned to take the time off to pursue some options he was thinking about lately.

Landon made sure the door's deadbolt and chain was on; he had no desire to have to deal with Shelly again tonight. A woman brazen enough to saunter in public naked could do anything.

What would he say to Candice when he arrived in Baton Rouge tomorrow night?

Candice.

He was excited and nervous about seeing her. What would it have been like to look through the peep hole to see Candice standing there in his pilot hat?

Landon had long since given up trying not to be attracted to her. She was gorgeous, had legs for days, and courage like he'd never seen. She was also still recovering from being in an abusive marriage and probably vulnerable as hell. But, for some reason he wasn't worried about convincing her to go on the trip, he was nervous about seeing her again.

Chapter 2

Lunch with Sophia

Sophia was already seated when he arrived at their favorite Italian restaurant. He stood back to watch a brave soul approach her at the table as she looked at the menu. Whatever the guy was trying to say couldn't have been too impressive, because Sophia didn't bother to even speak. She looked up over her reading glasses and darted the guy a look that said "don't even try it."

"Now how in the world are you ever going to meet a husband if you keep scaring men off like that?" Sophia's glare immediately softened to a welcoming smile as she stood to give Landon a hug.

"A husband? Now what in the world would I ever do with one of those?" She stood back to get a good look at him. "I do believe that even if we were the last two people on earth, we would still shun monogamy."

"What? You don't think I would be exciting enough for you?"

"Aw hush darling and sit down. I'm starving. Where have you been? You weren't trying to bag one of your flight attendants on my time, were you?" They sat across from each other.

"Now would I do that? I'm a respectable pilot and it wouldn't look good if I were fraternizing with my staff."

"Would and have. Now, how have you been? I haven't seen you in ages. Catch me up on everything."

"It *has* been a while since I've seen you, hasn't it?" He reached for the glass of water the waiter placed on the table and took a sip. "Well, Joshua got married about six months ago to woman he met in New Orleans while he was there teaching at Loyola. Now, they are taking an extended honeymoon sailing around on the *Phoenix*, the yacht Joshua recently had built.

"Married! How is the ice princess taking the news?"

"Yes, married."

" I'm just glad he didn't marry that stuck up bitch, Victoria." Victoria was the woman Landon's mom handpicked for Joshua

"I am pleased to say, my mom, the ice princess as you so accurately call her, did not take it well. She finally consented to accept the marriage but was hell bent on taking over the wedding so she could pass Alex off as some uppity debutante with a pedigree, I suppose. Alex was having none of that and opted for a private ceremony with only myself and her friend Candice in attendance."

"Southern girl huh, how come I haven't heard you mention her before? I didn't even know Joshua was seeing anyone."

"He wasn't. He'd only known her about five or six days before he was confessing to me how much he loved her and how he'd made a mistake by not telling her so, before he left. He'd had a lot to say during that particular meeting. He also felt the need to tell me I was a coward, a callous bastard and the only reason why I go out with so many women is because I don't want to end up like our father."

"Which is?"

"A man who lets his wife dictate his life." Landon's brow furrowed and he gave a short scoff, "Can you believe he said that?"

"It would explain a lot."

"Eh too, Sophia." Landon dropped his menu and pushed back slightly from the table. "I can't believe you would say something like that to me. I thought we were one of a kind."

"Why are you getting so upset, Landon?"

"My best friend thinks I'm a callous bastard."

"I didn't say that at all. I just said it would explain a lot."

Landon wasn't in the mood to get into an argument with Sophia; he usually didn't win.

"Can we change the subject please? I don't have the strength for an argument. I'll need to save it all for the one I'm sure to have with Candice."

Sophia sat back in her seat, scooted her glasses further down on her nose and gave Landon an appraising look. "Since when does the great Landon Phoenix argue with women?" She patted her chest lightly, "Present company excluded of course." Landon knew he'd made a mistake the moment he mentioned Candice's name. Sophia was like a bloodhound. When she picked up on even a hint of a scent of something, her nose dragged the ground until she found the source.

"Calm down, Dick Tracey. I just told you, Candice is my sister-in-law's best friend," he said as if that explained everything.

The waiter came to take their orders and he hoped that the distraction would send her on another trail. No such luck.

"Why is it you'll find yourself in an argument with her?"

Landon simply dropped his head in defeat. He knew there was no way he would be able to get around talking about Candice. So he told her.

By the time their food arrived, he had relayed the entire story of how he accidently met Candice and Alexandra in the Boston airport when Alex spilled a cup of coffee on him. It was a total coincidence that she turned out to be the woman his brother only recently mentioned he had fallen in love with. Alex was in town for a job interview with a prominent law firm and Candice was traveling with her. It was as simple as that.

Candice on the other hand was not as simple. It turned out that she was traveling with Alex because she'd only recently left her abusive husband. Landon found out about the husband while they were having dinner on their first night in Boston. It was like a physical blow to him when he found out that someone had actually put their hands on such a beautiful woman other than to make love to her.

He immediately knew that she would not be just some woman he could toy with, but it didn't bother him at all. Over the course of the few days they'd been in Boston, Candice and Landon set out to get Joshua and Alex back together and in doing so, they formed a special friendship. That was eight months ago and he hadn't been able to stop thinking about her.

They ate lunch including dessert. Sophia was really excited about the new dance studio she was opening in Manhattan. Her list of clientele was quite impressive. Landon was always amazed when she mentioned some of the famous names that took lessons from her, but Sophia didn't cater to "superstar" attitudes and whims. She was the best Latin dance instructor in town and everyone knew it. They also knew she treated everyone the same. She didn't care how much money or fame they had.

Landon was glad the conversation shifted away from him. He wasn't ready to answer a lot of questions about Candice or his feelings about his father. He wasn't even sure if he could answer them.

"Candice huh?"

"Huh….What?" He asked looking confused.

"Aww Landon, stammering is not attractive. It's not even you. Now what is the deal with this Candice woman? What does she do anyway?"

"You're not going to let this go are you?" He smiled at her, already knowing the answer.

"Why should I? We have no secrets from each other and the very fact that I'm having to pull this out of you is speaking volumes my dear friend."

She returned his smile with one of her own. It was the same smile that drew a person to her gorgeous

28

lips and attracted him to her in the first place. It was also the very one that she used as a weapon to get what she wanted.

"Easy Sophia, you can put your big guns away. Her name is Candice Freedman, and like I said before, she is my sister-in-law's best friend from Baton Rouge, Louisiana."

"I thought you said Joshua was teaching at Loyola."

"I did."

"Then how did he meet his wife...umm...what's her name...Alex?"

"Yes, Alexandra, but we call her Alex. She's also from Baton Rouge, but she was living in New Orleans while attending Loyola to get her law degree. Now can I get back to Candice?"

"Yes, please do."

"Candice is an artist and works in an art gallery there in Baton Rouge. Her birthday is coming up and Alex has somehow convinced me to travel there to make her go on a trip Joshua and Alex purchased for her. Everything is already set up. She has an entire itinerary of guided tours that will only increase her appreciation of art. I guess they figure she needs to get away. I believe she is now divorced or close to it."

"And you said that her husband was a wife beater?"

"Yes."

"That bastard."

"Yes."

Landon and Sophia talked for a few minutes longer, but she didn't ask him anymore questions about Candice. Most of their visits were usually just long enough for lunch or dinner.

She told him she would surprise him in London one day soon when they both had time off. Neither knew when that would be, because she was always dancing and he was always flying. He gave his friend a big kiss and hug before they each went their separate ways again. Landon was scheduled to fly to Baton Rouge in less than two hours and he couldn't help but wonder what it was going be like to see Candice Freedman again.

Chapter 3

The Proposition

"So what do you think of my proposition?" Landon was nearly floored when he walked into the art gallery and found Candice standing there with her hands on her hips in a skirt that hugged her beautiful round backside with perfection. She had on the sexiest pair of boots he'd ever seen. They had a high skinny heal and zipped up the back to the top just below her knees. She looked very chic and a little edgy—he loved it. Her back had been to him, but he would have known her anywhere. He'd seen her tall, fine, frame in his dreams on many occasions. She wasn't just his fantasy, she was *the* fantasy.

"Proposition? Is that what they are calling it now?"

"What would you call it?"

"I would call it what it is…an ultimatum." She had that hand on her hip again, but there was something in her eyes he hadn't seen before—fire. She was fired up and it revved him up like a car at the Daytona 500.

"That's not what it's meant to be."

31

"Well, Mr. Phoenix, I don't know what world you live in, but in mine, when someone tells you that you either go gallivanting, alone, mind you, all over Europe or they will insist that their newly married best friend leave her husband to come babysit her poor pitiful friend; I don't know what else you would call it." She dropped her hand from her hip like a spoiled child. "And I can't believe they sent you here, all the way from London, to try to make me go!"

"First of all you've totally misunderstood me and by no means do I now, or would ever, consider you pitiful. I'm here because I promised myself the next time I came to the states and I had some time off, I would come to visit you. I spoke to Alex recently and she told me you were just finishing up a show, so I took the chance that you were in town." He could see her softening a little, but he knew he still had a lot of convincing to do.

"Yes, I am just finishing up a show, so there's no way I can leave town right now, Landon."

"Do you physically have to be here to handle the rest of the details?"

"No, but…"

"So you could leave if you wanted to?"

"Landon, I know it sounds like the greatest opportunity in the world, to go touring Europe, but it's not something I want to do alone." He could tell she was trying to focus her eyes on anything but him and took that as a good sign.

"You won't be alone; I'll be with you as your own personal tour guide." He hadn't planned on saying that to her. The words just shot out of his mouth. Candice touring Europe alone wasn't something he wanted her to do either. Alex and Joshua promised to meet her in Italy for a week, but that still left her traveling by herself for two weeks.

"Landon, I..."

"Just think about it. I'm going to my hotel now to shower and change. We can talk about it more over dinner if you like. I can pick you up from your apartment or will you still be here?" He braced himself for an objection to dinner.

"I'll still be here." He knew she was about to say more, but he wasn't going to give her an opportunity to turn him down.

"Ok, then I'll pick you up in about an hour and a half. Will that give you enough time to finish up things here?"

"Yes."

"Ok, I'll see you in a little while." He quickly hugged her, kissed her on her cheek and went back out to his rental car before his confident gait was betrayed by his knees beginning to buckle beneath him.

It took Candice a moment before she could move her feet to go back to her office. Her work seemed to be a permanent fixture in the gallery lately and so was she. Somehow she was slowly taking on some of the responsibilities of running the gallery. She sat at her desk still not believing that Landon Phoenix was in Baton Rouge and had just been in to see her. Seconds before she'd heard his voice, she had been thinking of him. He didn't notice the painting she was looking at when he walked in. It was one she'd actually done for him.

She also couldn't believe what he was proposing to her. Would he actually spend three weeks in Europe with her? She was dying to go to Europe since she and Alex met, but she never considered going there without her.

Alex had a husband and a new life now. Though she knew they would always be friends and loved each other like sisters. Especially after their estrangement when Candice's husband forced her to break all ties with her friends and most of her family.

Candice had to abandon her friendship with Alex and it broke her heart. Her husband Devin was convinced that other women were jealous of their marriage and would try to break them up. She was a staunch believer that the husband was the head of the household so she did what he asked.

Her parents, William and Lillian Carwin, were a living example for her. They loved and respected each other, and although her mother was very stubborn and outspoken about many things, she always yielded to her husband's wishes if he deemed his contrasting view was best for the family. She knew her dad often let her mom have her way, just as she knew her mom catered to her dad's ego by letting him have the final say on the few things they disagreed on. Naturally, yielding to her husband's wishes was what she thought she was supposed to do; it was what she saw her mother do.

However, Candice found out that all marriages were not like the example she'd seen all her life. Soon after her marriage to Devin she realized that not only was she isolated from people that cared about her, but she traded her education and dreams for a life in hell. For eight years she was victim to his mental and physical abuse. On the outside they were an ideal couple, but privately she was constantly walking on a rotten bridge suspended over a lake of lava—one wrong move and she was done for.

The night she got the courage to leave him was the night of her very first art show. She was allowed to paint after her husband's boss discovered how talented she was when he saw a painting on the wall of their home. That same night was also the first time she saw Alex following eight long years. Devin was drunk and physically assaulted Alex when she refused his advances. Joshua promptly kicked his ass and when Candice came upon the scene, she too, had to be pulled off of him.

Candice knew then, that she would never be able to walk back into the gates of hell with Devin Freedman again. She knew she had to leave him, but making the decision to divorce him did not come right away. When she married Devin, she made a promise to God and her parents that she would be married to him forever. It wasn't until she found out that he was involved in numerous affairs during their marriage that she made the decision to divorce him. She'd had an excellent lawyer who convinced Devin and his attorney not to contest the divorce or all the sorted details of his affairs would be made public. Unethical behavior in any form was not appealing to clients of investment bankers.

It took about six months for the divorce to be final. In fact she got the final paperwork, including the documents to change her name back to Candice Carwin, only a week ago. It was the same day she received the gift from Joshua and Alex disguised as a birthday present. She knew that it actually was a get-out-of-town-because-you-are-finally-free present.

Could she actually spend three weeks traveling with Landon? What would people think?

Candice placed some files in a box to be put in storage. Why should she care what people thought? If she decided to go on the trip with him, it would be her decision and hers alone. Just thinking about it made tingling sensations climb up the insides of her thighs, which shocked her. She shook the feeling off and attributed it to the excitement of just the possibility of the trip.

The gallery door was locked when Landon returned. He knocked on the door and was greeted by a very slender man wearing a three-piece suit and bow tie. He obviously expected Landon, because he greeted him by name and told him Ms. Carwin would be with him in a moment.

"Carwin?" Landon said to himself. He thought maybe that was Candice's maiden name, and if she was being addressed by that name, then she must be divorced. Relief gently relaxed tension in his jaws and shoulders that he wasn't aware he had. Just knowing Candice was no longer tied to Devin strengthened his will to convince her that traveling through Europe with him, was the perfect plan.

Landon didn't noticed earlier, but he was impressed with the gallery's design and layout. It was very modish without being cold and sterile as some galleries seem to be. There were little benches placed in front of much of the artwork with a maze of walls and vaulted ceilings, giving the appearance of privacy without being closed in. Landon strolled through the gallery glancing at the artwork. It was his first time seeing any of Candice's work. He knew his brother and wife owned several pieces, and always spoke of how talented she was.

He was awe struck by the raw emotions that poured from each painting. He couldn't speak if he wanted to. She was simply amazing. From the moment he'd met Candice, she was the epitome of elegance, grace and strength. She was, to put it simply, a classy lady. And to have all this talent stored inside her was absolutely remarkable.

He couldn't imagine how a woman with so much going for her could let a man physically and mentally abuse her. Every painting seemed to have its own story to tell.

Landon gasped. He reached to touch it, but stilled his hand as if it would disappear if he touched it. It was a painting of the sun rising, casting a golden glow over the clouds, as seen from the perspective of an airplane cockpit. He had viewed scenes like it, many times flying over the Atlantic. It was one of the reasons he loved to fly. He always thought some of the views he was privy to, were unlike any masterpieces a mere human could create.

He couldn't believe it. A human had actually duplicated one. The image Candice captured on her canvass was one Landon knew he would never forget. It had made him feel as if God was sharing a secret with him that day and for some reason, when he landed, he called and told Candice about it.

Landon couldn't believe she actually captured the essence of that morning just from the description he'd given her. He was stunned, not only that she had the ability to do it, but that she had done it at all. His heart was racing and he wasn't sure why.

"So, do you like it?"

He still couldn't take his eyes off of it and spoke without turning towards her. "It's amazing. It's as if you were inside my mind."

"Well if I'd been inside your mind, I would have known you would be in Baton Rouge." She moved closer to him. "I did that one for you. You're welcomed to take it when you leave."

He turned to face her. "You did it for me?... But why?... Don't you want to sell it? I'm sure you've had many offers." Landon was almost stumbling over the words falling out of his mouth.

"It's not mine to sell. It's your scene; I just put it on the canvas for you."

Landon didn't know what to say and for a moment couldn't say anything.

"Thank you Candice. You're incredible."

"Well you're not getting off that easy. I'm going to make you buy me a big fancy meal."

"Gladly," he said and gently took her hand as they walked towards the door.

Chapter 4

The Answer

Landon Phoenix was the type of man that could look sexy wearing footed pajamas cradling a teddy bear. So Candice couldn't blame the curly-head waitress for looking at him with her eyes blinking in slow motion while she was telling *her* about the chef's specials for the day.

Candice knew Landon was handsome, but she often wondered what drew women to him like a beetle to a bug zapper. She took a moment to look at him while he tried hard to pretend Curly Top's shameless flirting was not bothering him.

He wore his hair cut close to his head so when you looked at him all you saw were those dazzling gray-blue eyes and a mouth that looked like it could do all sorts of wicked things to you. It was in the eyes, she thought. They looked as if they could see your secrets and weren't bothered by them. The flecks of gray flickered like a diamond solitaire. She loved that he was tall. She could wear high heels without being taller than him. And there were something about his hands

41

that caught her attention the first time she saw him in the airport the day Alex spilled coffee on him.

He had reached to shake her hand and she liked the fact that he didn't insult her by giving her one of those dainty tea-time handshakes that many men feel obliged to give those of the "weaker" sex. He took her hand in his and it felt firm, strong, and safe. The contrast of his light skin mingled with her chestnut tone was a novelty to her. Though she had no idea who he was at the time, she sensed then, that she could be safe in this man's hands.

Candice was so caught up in her appreciation of Landon's features that she hadn't realized the waitress was gone and Landon was talking to her. She assumed he was asking her if she was ready to order.

"Yes." She said giving her menu one final look and tried to refocus on her surroundings. There was a soft glow of light over each table like lightning bugs had gathered to hear the whispered conversations. She loved restaurants that used actual table linens. There were small clear glass vases arranged with a half dozen deep red roses on each table and soft music playing in the background of googly-eyed lovers soft conversations.

This probably wasn't the ideal place to discuss Landon's outrageous proposal, but she was hungry and the restaurant was across the street. Besides, she felt kind of giddy about being in such romantic surroundings with Landon. The fact that the waitress flirted with him and he ignored her, made her feel flattered that he was sitting there with her and not some other woman. Candice looked at him again, confirming the fact that the man was downright toe-curling sexy.

"Yes?" He asked, a little surprised.

"Yes, Landon I'm ready." She placed her menu to the side and looked up into Landon's smiling face. "She must have promised you something really special to have you grinning like that." Candice said looking from him to the waitress coming back to the table with two glasses of wine.

"She did, actually, and I can't wait to leave. How long will it take you to get packed?"

"Packed?"

"Yes packed. That's what people normally do before a vacation. Or had you planned on just bringing that little number you have on? Either way is fine with me, though you may need a heavier coat, especially since we will have to stop in London."

Candice had no idea what Landon was rambling on about, but had the sneaking suspicion that she may have missed something in their conversation.

43

"We were talking about ordering, right?"

"Wrong my friend." He knew she wasn't paying any attention to him and took the opportunity to slip in the question of her going to Europe with him. "You just agreed to allow me to travel to Europe with you and there is no way I'm letting you get out of it now. And if you didn't know what I was talking about, then what could possibly have had your attention so diverted?"

Landon took a sip of wine, placed the glass back on the smooth white tablecloth and sat back in his seat with a child-like innocence of a kid bringing his mom a flower picked from her prize winning rose bush.

She had been duped. She could lie and say she was thinking about something at the gallery, but he had a way of reading her that made it impossible not to tell him the truth. For some reason, she found out after meeting him, he was acutely perceptive of her. So she either tell him that she was secretly checking him out or agree that she knew what they'd been discussing.

"I'll need a couple of days to finish up some things at the gallery and be ready to go."

———

Landon walked to the window and looked out at the sky; he couldn't even see the lights from the planes he knew were flying above. He walked to the mini bar, pulled out an eight-dollar beer and took a long cold swig of it then fell into the chair at the desk in the suite he'd been in since arriving in Baton Rouge.

What had him on edge?

There was really no need to wonder about it, because he knew exactly why he couldn't sit still. They would be on a plane to London in less than twelve hours and she had been so busy at the gallery that he hadn't seen her since the night they went to dinner. Time was moving at the speed of a New York City traffic jam and at any moment he was afraid Candice would call to tell him she changed her mind.

He started and nearly dropped his beer when the phone in his pocked began to vibrate. Landon's chest tightened and his pulse quickened a little as he fished his phone out of his pocket. It was Joshua. He relaxed, then immediately wondered if maybe Candice told Joshua to tell him she no longer wanted to go.

"Hello."

"What's up Big Bro? You answered the phone like you were expecting it to be the police or something. Everything all right?"

45

"Yea, I'm fine. Just was caught up in a movie."
He lied. "How are you and my beautiful sister-in-law
and where are you?"

"We're fine and we're still in Bermuda...So,
how did it go? Were you able to convince her to go on
the trip?"

"Now has your brother ever let you down?"

"You mean she's going to go? When?"

Landon could hear Alex clapping and cheering
in the background. She picked up another receiver and
offered her thanks. Landon walked over to the window
again.

"Yes she is going to go on the trip." He closed
his eyes and paused a moment. "As a matter of fact, we
leave in the morning." He looked up at the sky again
and added, "That is, if the weather holds out."

"We!" Joshua and Alex exploded at the same
time.

"Yes, we." He picked up the beer again and
realized it was empty. "I have some time off and
offered to join her." There was silence on the phone.
Landon imagined them just standing there looking at
each other like someone just told them the bird got out
with the cat in the house.

Joshua finally spoke.

46

"So....*you're* going *with* her? You'll be with her the entire time?"

Landon pulled the phone away from his ear and just looked at it like he was checking to see if he still had a connection.

"Yea, man...what's the problem?"

"And Candice agreed to go *with.... you*?" It was Alex that spoke that time.

"What's wrong with the two of you? You act like she's about to get in the chariot with Hades or something." Silence again. "Look you two, I don't know what you're thinking but it's not like that. Candice refused to go alone. I know she really needs to get away so I volunteered to go with her."

"We're sorry Landon," Alex said finally. "We didn't mean to insinuate anything. We are just...well...surprised I guess. We're glad that C.C. won't be alone. You will take good care of her won't you Landon?" There was something in Alex's tone that told Landon she was worried about more than Candice's safety.

"Of course I will." And he meant it. They chatted a few more minutes about their travels aboard their yacht and when Alex hung up her receiver, Landon and Joshua talked about the transformation their dad made since Joshua's birthday party when their parents initially met Alexandra. He no longer seemed to be a hen-pecked husband. When Landon hung up the phone, he still couldn't help but feel as if his father's new stance with his mother may have come too late.

The phone rang again the moment he put it back into his pocket. It was Candice. He started to ignore the call just in case she had changed her mind, but knew he couldn't do that.

"Hey Lady, you need me to come over and help you sit on your suitcase?" He closed his eyes and held his breath.

"Actually I might, but I'm not done packing yet." She said. A quiet sigh escaped him and a smile lit his face as he sank back into the chair at the desk.

"You sound like you're relieved."

"I am. I thought you were calling to tell me you changed your mind," he said, "but I'm so glad you didn't."

There was silence on the phone.

"Hello?"

"Ummm… sorry…. for a moment I'd forgotten what I was calling about. I was thinking that since we need to be at the airport so early that it would be more convenient if you picked me up tonight and I'll just get a room where you are. Then we can just leave from the hotel. What do you think?"

"That's fine with me Candice, but there's no sense in you getting another room. You can stay here with me. You can have the bedroom and I'll sleep on the sofa."

"Are you sure?"

"Positive. How long before you're ready?"

"Well, I was going to run out to pick up something to eat then finish packing...About an hour and a half or so, but you can come over now and I'll pick you up something too. Have you eaten?"

Landon had already stood, grabbed his rental car keys and stuffed his hotel key into his back pocket.

"No, I haven't eaten yet. How about you go ahead and continue packing, I'll pick up something for us both and head on over there? That way, by the time I get there you'll be ready for me to sit on the suite case. And by the way, you better make sure you have something really warm to wear tomorrow because the forecast says it's going to be really cold and you know you Southerners aren't used to really cold weather."

"Ok, Landon, that sounds perfect. I'll make sure I'm dressed warmly. My mom is convinced it is going to snow soon."

"Is she? Why?"

"She says she can feel the snow coming. She has a sense about things…Don't ask. It's weird I know. Anyway, see you in a little while. And anything you get is fine with me. I'm so hungry I could devour anything at this point."

Landon tried like hell to get the image of her devouring him, out of his head, but for the life of him he couldn't get it to budge.

Chapter 5

The Encounter

Candice got up early to shower and get ready before Landon needed the bathroom. All she needed was to see him walking through the bedroom to the bathroom in his boxers. She'd already been on edge since they arrived to his hotel room.

Everything he did just dripped sexy and she found herself wanting to hold her tongue out and wait for a drop to land on it. *Good Lord!* How in the world would she ever make it an entire three weeks with this man without appearing to be some sort of floozy?

From the moment they'd met, even after the whole ordeal of Devin still clinging to her, she was attracted to Landon. When he suggested he travel with her, she was scared to death that he would somehow know that she'd been dreaming about him since the last time they saw each other at the wedding.

The wedding was over and they were disembarking from the *Phoenix*, Joshua's new yacht, and she slipped and fell right into Landon. He caught her and held her for a moment like he didn't want her to move away, and in fact, she didn't want to move away. He was behind her and she landed smack against his chest. His hands firmly on her waist, he whispered in her ear, "Are you ok?" Never had any man sounded so delicious to her. She couldn't speak. She just nodded her head and prayed she would be able to stand on her own accord once his hands fell away from her.

Until they were safely on the other boat, he placed his hand lightly on the small of her back to steady her. Sweet Lord, everywhere he touched felt good.

When Candice arrived at the door of the hotel room, Landon placed his hand in the exact spot on her back as he had the day of the wedding, to lead her into his suite. If she closed her eyes, she could still feel it there. She could still breathe in the subtle, yet alluring cologne he wore, causing her to feel something soft, safe, and sexy, tingling up her spine, traveling around her shoulders, over her breasts and leaving her nipples hard and longing for something she was sure only Landon Phoenix could supply.

Ms. Floozy just would not go away.

It was just about 4:30 am and she wanted to run down to the lobby and grab something to eat for the both of them. There was a café/market near the lobby that stayed open twenty-four hours.

She turned off her light before she opened the bedroom door so she wouldn't wake Landon. He still had a few minutes to sleep before he needed to get up. With stealth movements she opened the bedroom door. It was so dark, she wondered if she would be able to find her way to the door that led to the corridor.

Candice took two steps and stumbled right smack into Landon.

"I'm sorry!" they both said simultaneously.

She noticed that his arms immediately went around her and held her tight the moment their bodies touched. She also noticed that his chest wasn't the only thing that was rock hard on him, but in spite of that, to steady herself her arms instinctively went around Landon and her hands flat against his back, felt his smooth bare skin. Grabbing him like she did was understandable (perhaps), but how she ended up with the side of her head resting on his shoulder, she was not aware.

That damn Floozy showed up again.

"You ok?" He asked.

"Uh huh. You?"

"Yes, I was just getting ready to wake you, but I see that you are already dressed and ready to go. You're not trying to duck out on me are you?"

His mouth was just at the level of her forehead and if she tilted her head up, her mouth, she was sure, would be able to taste his.

The light flicked on and she realized her body was draped around Landon like an apron and felt her face heat with embarrassment. She pulled away from him and for the tiniest of moments, felt some resistance. *Was that her imagination?*

Candice stood back with a crooked smile and a sheepish look in her eyes and quickly told him where she was going before she bolted out of the door.

Landon stood in the shower with his hands resting against the tile in front of him, letting the water try to pound some sense into his head. He could still smell the lavender shower gel she used. He'd inhaled it before. It was a fragrance she used often.

What was he doing? He told himself that Candice was off limits the moment Alex mentioned she wanted him to talk to her. Now he was losing sleep again like he did right after he'd met her.

Usually he could fall asleep anywhere; it was the nature of his job that gave him the ability. So sleeping on the sofa was a nonfactor. Being able to adjust quickly to time differences and get sleep when he could, was a necessity to be well rested and able to do his job at 100%, but just knowing there was only a door that separated him from Candice kept him awake most of the night.

A half hour of sound sleep was all he managed before something woke him. He thought he may as well get her up in case she was one of those women that needed extra time to do whatever it was that they did in the mornings.

Landon walked towards the bedroom in the dark wondering if she was a heavy sleeper and if he would have to gently nudge her awake. Candice was asleep in his hotel room. There were so many ways he could think to wake her and in most of the scenarios her back was nuzzled into his front. Just thinking about it made him as hard as granite. He reached for the doorknob wondering if it was locked and she was suddenly in his arms.

Was he still asleep? Just in case, he figured he would hold on to her a moment. It all happened so quickly. One moment he was thinking about all the scandalous ways he could wake her and the next moment she was stumbling into his arms.

Had he imagined her head lying on his shoulder and her arms holding him tightly?

Landon was taken by surprise, but nevertheless he loved the way she felt in his arms—like she belonged in them. When she tried to pull away from him he just held on to her.

Landon slammed the palm of his hand against the tile, feeling like an idiot. He was positive he offended her by the way she ran out so quickly. She must surely think he was the quintessential playboy everyone claimed him to be.

Landon checked his watch as he stood at the window looking out, waiting for Candice to return. She left nearly twenty minutes ago. What was taking her so long? He knew he shouldn't have let her go down there by herself. Landon grabbed the room key and walked towards the door just as she walked in. He was surprised because she wasn't carrying anything.

"Was it still closed?" She just stood there and stared at him.

"Candice?" She quickly shook her head from left to right.

"Candice what's wrong?" He didn't think she was answering his question. It was more like she was trying to rid her mind of something.

A tear slipped down her face.

"Candice, wha—" He took a step towards her and she quickly held up a hand to stop him. He stopped.

"I'm fine. I'm just tired." She slapped the wetness from her face and lifted the corners of her mouth in an effort to smile.

Landon was not fooled. Something was wrong and he had an idea what it was.

"Candice, I'm not crazy. You're upset and I'm sorry."

She rubbed her eyes with her hands and took a deep breath. He continued,

"It's my fault. You just took me by surprise this morning, that's all."

She frowned, confused. "Huh? What are you talking about Landon?"

"You rushed out of here so fast…"

He saw her confused look and realized that *he* wasn't the issue. He started towards her again and she purposely avoided him by stepping aside and walking past him. He turned and stared at her. She wiped her face again.

"You're crying. Why?"

She said nothing. He didn't know what was going on with her but he sure as hell was going to find out. Landon walked up behind Candice. He stood there not sure what to do or what to say.

57

"What is it?" He breathed the words trying not to disturb the silence but wishing it would end. Candice sobbed softly.

"What's wrong? What's wrong Candice?...Tell me." She didn't say a word, just turned, put her arms around his neck and cried. Landon held her tightly, his heart racing with worry. Something or someone upset her when she went downstairs and he needed to find out what or who.

Landon just held her and let her cry. She said nothing, pressed her body into his and buried her face into his neck.

Landon held her but was at a loss. He was completely caught off guard by her behavior. He wanted to pick her up and take her back to the rumpled bed she'd slept in, but knew this was not the time.

"Candice what's the matter? What happened? Did someone hurt you?" He pushed her away from him so he could look into her face.

"I'm sorry Landon...I just...he was so....awful." The last word was followed by another quiet sob.

"What 'he'? Who was awful to you? What happened Candice?"

Landon realized he was nearly shouting at her which was making her more upset. He pulled her close again and slowly rubbed her back.

"It's ok Candice. You're ok. I won't let anyone hurt you." He could feel her relaxing, but he was anything but relaxed. His blood was nearly boiling and it was taking every bit of strength that he had to stay calm for her. All he knew was that someone upset her to the point of crying.

Then he wondered if she was just still really fragile from the ordeal she lived through and could become upset over just about anything that might remind her of what her husband had put her through.

Landon placed his hands on her waist and stepped back. She looked up at him and he cupped her face wiping away a tear with his thumb. She put her head down.

"Candice you don't have to be embarrassed by a few tears, but I'm really concerned about why they are there. Please tell me what happened." He walked her over to the sofa and they sat down.

"It was Devin."

"Your ex-husband, Devin?"

"Yes, I saw him in the lobby."

Landon immediately stood.

"What did he do to you? If that bastard put his hands on you again…" She stood, grabbed his hand and looked up at him.

"He didn't hurt me…not physically anyway. I feel so stupid for letting him get to me." She put her head down again.

Landon didn't like the way she kept putting her head down as if she had something to be ashamed of. He reluctantly sat down with her, because what he really wanted to do was to find that bastard and show him what happens when someone fights back, but instead he pulled her close to him again and just held her there for a while. They needed to get going but he had to know what Devin said to her to make her cry. He knew that if he ever got the chance he would make Devin Freedman feel every ounce of pain he ever inflicted upon Candice.

"What happened?" He whispered.

"He walked into the café as I was leaving. It was the first time I'd seen him since the divorce." She paused a moment. She still had her head against his shoulder and he could smell the hint of lavendar from her hair.

"What did he say to you? Why is he even here, in a hotel?"

"My lawyer told me his firm transferred him to the Houston office soon after the incident at the art gallery. I guess he travels back and forth often because some of his clients are still here."

Landon remembered Candice telling him about Devin attacking Alexandra in the art gallery when they had dinner for the first time. It was what confirmed her decision to leave him.

Landon's jaw clenched as he braced himself for what Candice would say next. All he really wanted to do was to find that low-life and rip him apart. He didn't really give a damn about the particulars. Whatever he did, however minuscule, was too much.

Landon gave her a little squeeze to let her know she was safe now. She continued.

"He was surprised to see me at first, wondering what I was doing in a hotel 'sneaking about' so early in the morning. When I told him it was none of his business what I did, he accused me of being a whore. When I reminded him that I wasn't the one out screwing everything in a skirt during our marriage he told me…" She sniffed and wiped her eye.

"Told you what Candice?" Landon squeezed the words out through clinched jaws and waited for her to speak again.

61

"… that if I had satisfied him in bed then he wouldn't have needed to have affairs." She paused for a long moment and he wondered if she would continue. "He also said that the only reason he let me stay around so long was to promote stability for his image and so that he could have someone to screw between his real women and that even a lousy lay was better than none at all."

The embarrassment she felt from what she'd just told Landon was overwhelming. She had been having all sorts of scandalous thoughts about him.

Landon...

The man every woman wanted—the man who could choose whomever *he* wanted, whenever he wanted. Yet, she knew for certain that she didn't have a snowballs chance in hell with him, especially after what Devin admitted to her.

Candice was nearly incoherent by the time she stopped talking and Landon was livid.

"I'm sorry. I'm a mess." She sniffed loudly. "Maybe this isn't the right time for the trip."

He looked around for a tissue, but didn't see any.

"I think it's the perfect time to leave town. You need a change of scenery."

She cried again in his arms and each tear that fell from made his heart literally hurt. How could someone upset this beautiful, kind woman? How was it possible to have her in your arms and not want to always have her there? How was it possible, he thought, that they would travel for nearly a month and she not know he was falling in love with her?

Chapter 6

The Kiss

"What's the matter Landon?" She noticed Landon kept going to the window looking up at the sky with a deep frown on his face. She walked over to the window with him, shuddered and rubbed her hands over her arms.

"Goodness, it's cold over here."

"I know, which means it must really be cold outside." He moved over so she could get a better look.

Candice squinted while looking down on to the part of the hotel parking lot that she could see.

"Is it raining?"

"I think it may be sleet." He lifted his eyes towards the sky. "*That* sky isn't looking too friendly today." She watched him pull out his cell phone.

"Do you think the flight will be delayed?"

"It's the Houston flight that I'm worried about. Like I said before, this area of the country isn't used to this kind of weather and I'm afraid the flight to London will be canceled if the weather is anything like it is here or worse."

"Canceled? When do you think we'll be able to leave?"

"I'm not sure. I'm trying to see if we can get a flight to New York instead, then we can catch a flight to Heathrow on my normal route later this afternoon."

Candice sat on the sofa and watched Landon call the airport. He mouthed to her that he was listening to a special recording about some flight delays and cancelations due to the weather. She turned the television to The Weather Channel to see if there was any information about flight delays or weather in Houston. Just as she turned to the station the meteorologist was reporting a freak ice storm that hit Houston causing power outages, traffic accidents, and there was even a report of two people found dead sleeping in a car.

"Well there goes our chances of leaving from Houston today. Look Landon… all flights have been canceled."

Landon clicked his phone off, walked over to where she was sitting and looked at the TV.

"Yea, I was afraid of that. I tried to get us a flight out today to New York, but all the flights were full. We can fly to New York tomorrow afternoon, and then fly out to London from there."

She looked up at him. "Well I guess since you haven't turned in your rental car yet, you can take me home."

That was the last thing he wanted to do. Just the idea of her leaving was filling him with a sense of loss he had never experienced before. He should have been glad to be able to take her home so he could clear his head and try to get a handle on what was happening to him.

What *was* happening to him? He didn't want to stop to rationalize it or to talk himself out of the way he felt about Candice. It was new and exciting. It was terrifying. It was also frustrating to be falling for a woman that he couldn't have.

She'd not only just gotten a divorce; she was getting out of a marriage that left her pretty battered on the inside. Just to think, she had a near melt down just from running into the guy. Granted, he said some terrible things to her, but what if he messed her up so badly, that she was unable to handle any kind of relationship with anyone.

Landon knew that this trip was going to be pure torture for him, because he wanted her. It was just that simple. He wanted Candice Carwin, but he knew she was not a woman to just take for the wanting. He wouldn't back out of the trip now, even if he had the desire to. She needed a friend and he was determined to be there for her.

"Candice there's no sense in dragging all your luggage back to your place. Just stay here again."

"I guess you're right. I can just get a room for the night."

She obviously had misunderstood Landon and his meaning of "here", so with as much effort as he could muster, he tried to make his voice sound as nonchalant as possible.

"Me and that sofa got along pretty well last night; it will be an awful shame if I had to leave it tonight to go back to the bed." Though he was thinking exactly that.

"You're sure Landon? I don't want you to get tired of me before we get started on the trip."

He reached down took her hand and gently pulled her up so she was standing directly in front of him. "Not a chance." He thought for sure he saw relief flicker across her eyes after he'd spoken. He just stood there and looked at her face for a moment. She smiled at him.

Candice's features were etched into his brain. Her naturally arched brows had finally relaxed again and her dark brown eyes seem to hold secrets. Secrets he wanted her to share with him. Her mouth, he tried not to even look at her lips, because if there were a hint of invitation in them, they would be in trouble.

"Candice?" Landon brushed his thumbs underneath her eyes where the tears spilled earlier.

"Yes?" She said, barely able to get the word out. His eyes sucked the breath from her every time she looked into them directly.

Landon leaned over, gently moved her hair away from her ear and whispered, "I'm hungry and you didn't bring back breakfast."

"Huh?" She blinked. "Breakfast?"

Landon stood back and smiled.

"Yes, breakfast. Aren't you hungry?"

Little explosions went off in her belly from the affects of his eyes and the smile that accompanied it.

"Candice."

"Yea?"

"Come on let's go downstairs and have breakfast. The restaurant should be opened by now."

Without waiting for a response, he took her hand and walked towards the door. "We can stop by the front desk and let them know we'll be staying another night." When she didn't reply he stopped and turned towards her. "You ok?"

"Yea, I'm fine Landon." She lied. Just touching him was tilting her world. He held her hand like he'd been doing it all of his life and her hand fit there like that's where it belonged.

He brushed her cheek with the back of his free hand and wondered if she was still upset about seeing Devin. "You do know that you'll always be safe with me don't you?"

Candice squeezed his hand unable to answer for the moment. She always felt safe with Landon. She smiled at him and somehow couldn't keep from putting her arms around his neck.

"Landon Phoenix, you're such a great friend. How in the world did I ever get along without you all my life?" She stood back and put her hand in his again. "C'mon I can go for some eggs, toast and grits."

He looked at her with a mock frown on his face.

"Grits? Sounds like something used to clean bathroom tile. You Southerners will eat anything."

"My dear friend, you have no idea what you're missing." She closed her eyes and licked her lips. "They're delicious."

Landon's legs would need help keeping him up if she didn't put that tongue back in her mouth. Why did his legs keep betraying him that way? He grabbed the doorknob to steady himself, and then he heard her say, "I'll let you taste mine."

For Christ's sake, he was only a flesh and blood man and could handle so much. Watching Candice sweep her tongue across her bottom lip after she just pressed her body against his with her hug was one thing too much for the moment.

In his head he was asking permission. In his head he was telling her he just couldn't help himself. In his head she belonged to him.

All these things were taking place in his head, but in reality, he let her hand go, put his arm around her waist and pulled her to him like it was his given right to do so, and with his own tongue he followed the same trail across her bottom lip that hers had just made.

Landon merely meant to get the taste of her mouth that he felt he needed in order to move forward from the spot he was stuck in and to move forward to be the friend he was so desperately trying to be. That's what he meant anyway. What happened from his thought process to actually carrying it out was lost to him the moment his mouth touched hers. Food was replaced with his hunger for Candice.

Slowly at first, he tasted her lips from corner to corner, but that only whet his appetite for her even more. Was it his imagination or did she readily open her mouth to him when his tongue sought to acquaint itself with hers.

He was almost delirious from the taste of her.

The kiss was hot, greedy, and passionate. When he heard her moan he was nearly mad with wanting her, causing him to plunge further and taste every delectable part of her mouth his tongue could reach. His heart was in overdrive and his head spun. Landon needed to pull away if only for the necessity of breathing.

Landon tore his mouth away from hers, but held on to her; needing the contact. He stroked her back as if the rhythmic motion would somehow allow them to gain control of their breathing. Never in his life had a kiss left him teetering on the brink of losing control. He could've easily made love to her right there by the door.

What was it about this woman, he thought, that caused such a reaction in him?

She was beautiful yes, but he had definitely been around beautiful women before. Even before they'd been introduced, he felt a connection with her and after all the months that passed since, he still felt it.

He was afraid to look at her. Afraid he would see the same hurt and disappointment there that Devin caused. At the moment he couldn't handle it if he realized he'd caused her any type of pain. He needed to say something. Anything, to explain what just happened between them, though he didn't know what happened.

Candice spoke before Landon got the chance. Her voice was a little muffled with her mouth speaking into the collar of his shirt.

"Well that sure as hell beats eggs, toast, and grits."

"It does, does it?"

"Mmmm…hmm. I can recognize a great kiss even if I've never had one, because I sure have never been kissed like that before."

She still hadn't moved. Landon placed his hands on her waist and took a step back to look at her face.

"So you're not angry with me Candice?"

"Angry? What woman in her right mind would be angry after a kiss like that?"

"Well should we at least talk about it?"

"What's there to talk about? You kissed me, I kissed you back. End of story. To be honest I would have been a little insulted if you hadn't tried to kiss me. I understand you have quite a reputation with the ladies." Her words flew out in a world wind. "It's who you are Landon. It's probably best that we got it out of the way before we started tramping across Europe together."

Landon just stared at her. She was so far off base that she might as well play another sport.

"I see you've been talking to my sister-in-law, but…"

"Come on Landon let's eat."

She didn't reach for his hand that time or he would have noticed the trembling. That kiss shifted something inside of her and she didn't know how much longer she could stand there and pretend it was no big deal.

Landon Phoenix was indeed a big deal, but she knew he was also a man that prided himself on not attaching himself to any woman, which was just as well. She was done being any man's puppet. It was time she pulled the strings in her own life. She had to admit though, she felt totally comfortable with Landon, but it was also what frightened her the most.

They were going down to breakfast, but she knew it didn't matter if the finest chefs in Louisiana prepared the meal; nothing would even come close to the taste of Landon Phoenix.

Chapter 7

Mr. and Mrs. Phoenix

"What did you think of the grits?" Candice looked at Landon expectantly." "Good huh?"

They both were relatively quiet at breakfast and Candice tried to come up with something to lighten the mood. Or at least that's what she told herself. What she was actually trying to do was focus on something besides the movement of Landon's mouth. He took a bite of bacon and the slow methodical movements of his jaws and lips were making her quite envious of that bacon. He seemed to savor every bite he took. She couldn't help but picture him savoring every single taste of her.

What would it be like to make love to someone that actually cared about how she felt or cared about her for that matter? Candice had the sudden need to cross her legs and tightly hold them in place. Landon would no doubt take care in pleasing her, but could she sleep with a man that was only sleeping with her to fulfill a sexual desire? No. She needed to get herself together. They would be traveling together for the next three weeks and if she didn't get some new thoughts quickly she would drive herself mad. Landon was a very good friend to her and she didn't want to jeopardize that by having a tryst with him even if he wanted to—which was doubtful after what she'd confessed to him about Devin.

Candice could tell Landon had something on his mind and it was no doubt the kiss they shared earlier. Maybe he was re-thinking the idea of going to Europe with her. Maybe he planned all along to have a brief affair with her and now realized that she wouldn't go along with it.

"Landon?" When he didn't answer she reached across the table and tapped her finger near his plate. "Earth to Landon."

"Yea, sorry, are you ready to go?" He removed the napkin from his lap and placed it on the table.

She frowned. "What's the matter with you? You haven't said two words to me the whole time we've been sitting at breakfast."

"I'm sorry Candice. I didn't mean to ignore you. I've just been thinking about the comment you made earlier."

"And what comment was that Mr. Phoenix?" She smiled at him to lighten the mood, but his face remained passive and there was seriousness in his eyes that she had never seen there before. She looked away from him, picked up her glass, took a sip and put it back on the linen covered table. She was fiddling with her spoon when she felt his hand on hers.

"That spoon is fine Candice. Look at me please." When she did, the blue-gray flecks in his eyes caused her breath to catch and lips to part slightly.

"Yes Landon?"

He had asked for it, but wasn't quite prepared for a direct onslaught of his senses. She looked directly at him and the vulnerability that showed on her face caught him off guard. His words froze on his tongue. Her voice was a soft silky sigh that made him instantly aroused and when he touched her on the hand she turned her palm up and gingerly wrapped her fingers around his. That simple gesture shot flames from the bottom of his feet to his groin. He wouldn't be able to get up from the table if the building was on fire.

He wanted to speak but his focus was locked on the lips that looked as if they were waiting for him to kiss them again. Instead of being able to move on after kissing her, he was now addicted and knew he would never tire of tasting this woman.

"Yes Landon, what is it? What comment did I make?"

He blinked and straightened his own spoon before he gathered his thoughts again to speak.

"You said I had quite a reputation with the ladies and that was who I was."

"Yea? And?"

"I think you have the wrong impression of me, in fact, you've never indicated to me that you thought I was some sort of ladies man. That's not who I am at all" He pulled his hand away and sat back. Candice looked down, fiddled with her spoon again, and smoothed out the ripple in the table cloth before she sat back in the chair and finally brought her eyes back up to meet Landon's.

"I guess that comment wasn't quite fair, was it?" Before he could answer Landon's cell phone rang. He pulled his phone out of his pocket, looked at the number, rolled his eyes and let out a long sigh. He hit the button and answered.

"Don't you think it's kind of early for a social call, Brother Dear?"

"It's Alex, and it's not too early because I know you had an early flight to Houston and we heard flights were canceled out of Houston. So what are you guys up to? And where is C.C.? I called her phone but she didn't answer. Did you talk to her this morning? Did you find out about the cancelation before you had

77

a chance to pick her up?" Landon looked at Candice then up at the ceiling waiting for a chance to speak. "Landon did you hear me?"

"Yes I heard you. I was just wondering which question you wanted me to answer first."

"Have you heard from C.C.?" she asked again.

"Yes." He answered but offered nothing further. He was deliberately toying with her.

"Are you still leaving today?"

"No, we're going to get a flight out to New York tomorrow if the weather holds. Now if you don't mind, I'd like to get back to what I was doing."

"And what was that?" Landon groaned at the question. You can take the lawyer out of the courtroom but you can't take the "nosey" out of the lawyer, especially his sister-in-law, he thought.

"Since you must know, I was in bed." He put his index finger up to his mouth so Candice would know not to say anything.

"In bed?"

"Yes."

"Where is C.C.?"

"Oh, she's right here…hold on." He passed the phone to Candice, "Here you go baby, Alex wants to talk to you." He could hear Alex yelling something as he passed the phone to Candice. Before Candice placed it to her ear, she mouthed to Landon, "You should be ashamed of yourself."

"Yes, Alex what is it dear?...No I'm not! We're sitting at breakfast... He was just playing with you." Alex must have asked her question after question because all Candice's replies were either yes or no. Candice looked at Landon as if to say "Thanks for getting me into this."

"Tell her that's what she gets for being so nosey." After about five minutes Candice disconnected the call and handed the phone back Landon.

"Landon Phoenix you are so bad, but I have to admit she deserved it." Candice rolled her eyes. "Ever since I've been living on my own again, she's been treating me like her little kid sister."

"She means well. She knows you've had a rough go of things and just cares about you. That's all...We all do." Their gazes held for a moment. Candice looked away still a little uncomfortable with his kind and caring words. More people were arriving for breakfast. She scanned the tables hoping Devin wasn't one of them and looked back at Landon.

"There's a fine line between caring and meddling... She almost had a heart attack when she thought we were in bed together." As soon as it came out of her mouth she regretted it. That was the last image she needed. "Come on, we better make sure we can stay another night."

Landon hadn't gotten the chance to talk about her impression of him, but decided to table it for the moment.

There were several people at the front desk when they arrived. It seemed they weren't the only ones with flight issues. There were several clerks working behind the desk but they had to wait for one to become available.

"Good morning, how may I help you?"

Just as they walked up to the desk to address the freckled faced clerk who looked barely old enough to be driving let alone working in a hotel on a school day, there was a man walking up to the clerk beside Freckles. Candice quickly walked around Landon to put Landon between her and the man. She held onto Landon's arm and he could feel her trembling.

"Candice what's the matter?"

She quickly looked at the man who was now looking at her and Landon, and then looked back up at Landon. Landon turned his head to see what she was looking at and saw the man looking at them and knew instinctively that it was Devin. He fought an urge to punch the bastard, glowered at him, gave Candice a reassuring smile and put his arm firmly around Candice's waist pulling her closer to him.

Freckles spoke again, "How may I help you Sir?"

"My wife and I," Candice looked up at Landon startled at first, and then her eyes softened to relief. Landon's eyes danced like they always did whenever he was being mischievous and gave her a smile that made her insides flutter. She smiled back to show her appreciation for his cunning thoughtfulness. Freckles, on the other hand just looked from him to her and cleared his throat.

"Sir?"

"I'm sorry, what's your name?" He looked at the name tag. "Sorry John, but that smile of hers distracts me sometime"

John's uneasy smile indicated that he knew what Landon meant but tried not to show too much appreciation of the woman's appearance. Landon tried to hide his grin, understanding John's dilemma.

"Like I was saying, my wife and I were supposed to leave today on our honeymoon and one of our flights was canceled." Landon knew Devin was listening and had in fact completely turned towards them when he mentioned the honeymoon.

"We were hoping there was availability for us to stay one more night." Landon gave Freckles his name and watched as he clicked around on his computer for a few seconds.

"I'm sorry Mr. Phoenix, but the suite you're in is booked for the next couple of weeks. I would move them to another room, but they specifically asked for that one. Since it's your honeymoon anyway, we can put you up in the honeymoon suite and I'll even give you the same rate you're already paying. How's that?"

"Is that OK with you Mrs. Phoenix?" Landon looked at Candice and she only shrugged her shoulders.

Devin walked away from the desk but they both saw him hanging off to the side pretending he was looking for something in his cell phone.

"Yes baby." She could play the part too. She placed her hand on Landon's cheek turning his face towards her and kissed him softly on the lips. "That sounds perfect."

Landon was about to really get into character when he heard Freckles clear his throat again. He looked up at John, then behind him at the other guests standing there looking at their watches, irritated that they were holding up the line. Landon turned to the people behind them and said, "Sorry, we're on our honeymoon." There were several people to offer their congratulations and even a few catcalls from others.

"Mr. and Mrs. Phoenix we'll send someone up to get your bags and take them to your new suite. Here's the keys and I apologize for the inconvenience of moving, but I'm confident that you will enjoy your new accommodations."

Landon stood waiting for the elevator with his arm around Candice's waist unable to believe that he just introduced her as his wife and it felt like the most natural thing in the world. What bothered him was the reason why he did it. When the ding from the elevator sounded, he sent Candice up and told her he forgot to ask John something. Not quite ready to end the charade, he kissed her before she got on the elevator. Damn he loved kissing her.

Landon stood in front of the elevator and stared at Candice. She stood in the middle of it, kissed her hand and blew it towards him. He pretended to catch it and put his hand over his heart. She smiled at him again, put her hands on her hips, and lifted her shoulder in a flirty pose. Landon wanted so badly to jump on that elevator, head up to the honeymoon suite and consummate their "marriage," but instead he watched the doors close and turned towards the lobby.

The atrium of the hotel was spacious yet still cozy and comfortable. Landon spotted Devin sitting in a chair in an expensive navy suit that had seen better days, going through some papers. He placed the documents in his brief case and walked over to the concierge stand.

The woman there giggled at something Devin said and Landon tried to look at Candice's ex-husband as if he didn't know anything about him. He was about average height for a man, which made him only a couple inches taller than Candice He wore a well groomed beard and could easily be a model in a JCPenny catalog or something like that. Just from the reaction of the concierge, Landon could tell the man must have a way with words. He wondered how long it would take before the charm wore off and his true colors came shining through.

Landon walked towards the Concierge's desk. Devin turned to leave and found Landon in his path. Trying to step past him and couldn't, Devin looked up, and smiled.

"Excuse me, do I know you?" Devin asked.

Landon knew that Devin knew exactly who he was. He took a moment to get a good look at the man. Though he appeared to be well polished from afar, on closer inspection Devin's frayed edges were apparent.

His face had the sagging listless look of a drunk and his suit carried the shine dirty clothes get when ironed.

"No, you don't know me. And I guarantee that you don't want to know me." The warm playfulness in Landon's tone was gone and replaced with a cold and exacting edge. "I understand that you had a conversation with my wife this morning." His jaw twitched as he stood as casually as he could with one hand in his pocket and the other along his side trying not to ball it into a fist.

"Ha ha ha ha...*your* wife?"

"Yes, *my* wife Candice."

"Seeing that we've only been divorced about five minutes, I had no idea she was re-married."

"Well she is, and I'm going to tell you this once..." Landon took a step towards Devin, looked down at him with his face only inches away. "If you ever come near my wife, speak to her, look at her, or cause her any kind of discomfort or pain again; when I'm done with you, I promise you're going to be begging for the tortures of hell."

Landon turned to walk away then turned back to Devin who was still rooted to the spot. He held up his index finger. "Remember, you get this warning once. Your days of manipulating and torturing her are over or you'll find out what it feels like when someone

85

fights back." Landon walked away eager to get back to his *wife* and their honeymoon suite.

Chapter 8

Family, Work or Me?

Simply beautiful.

Landon stared at Candice fast asleep on the sofa with her head propped on one of the throw pillows. Reports of the weather mingled with a soft rumble, let him know that Candice was really tired. Beautiful, he thought again. Every time he saw her he wanted to hold her. With her lying on the sofa sound asleep, she seemed so vulnerable. He wanted to gather her into him and just feel the rhythms of her as she slept.

Landon noticed their bags gathered by the door. *That was fast*, but then remembered they were already packed and ready to go. There was a bottle of champagne chilling on the table near the window and he also remembered they were in the honeymoon suite, though it should have been obvious because of the massive tub that divided the bathroom from the main area. That would be interesting he thought.

Landon looked at Candice and for more than a moment he imagined an actual honeymoon with her. What would life be like with Candice? To come home from work and find her there; how would they greet each other?

Work.

There were times that Landon was away from home for days at a time. As a matter of fact, he found himself sleeping in hotel beds more often than his own. However, he knew pilots who were married. Their lifestyle worked out for them, whether it was because they couldn't wait to get home to their wife or because they were glad to be away. He couldn't imagine Candice being home at night alone without him.

Sophia was agonizingly close to the truth when she suggested Landon was ready to settle down. He wouldn't go as far to say that he was ready for the whole package: wife, kids, house, and dog. But meeting and sleeping with women all over the world no longer had the same appeal. He was finding himself turning down opportunities simply because he wanted more than sex. Sure there were several women who wanted a relationship, but he had yet to meet one that he wanted to spend more than a night at a time with.

Landon didn't want to wake Candice and he didn't want to disturb the perfection of the bedding, but he wanted to be near her so he slipped off his shoes and sat on the floor near her head. It was rare that he had a chance to sit and watch television just because it was on. Normally he was checking it for the weather or getting frustrated with subtitles that moved along too quickly when he was in foreign countries and didn't speak the language. So it was quite a novelty to sit and search for a movie to watch and actually have time to watch it.

There was a soft sigh from Candice before she adjusted herself a little on the sofa and her hand fell across his shoulder. Instinctively he closed his eyes, leaned his cheek against it and inhaled the soft lavender that floated around her.

Landon thought about what she'd said about him earlier. That he had a "reputation with the ladies." What the hell was that supposed to mean. *That she thought he had a string of women at his disposal?* Well he did actually, but he specifically chose women who were not looking for a relationship. There were a few who eventually wanted one but he never led them on and was always honest and straight forward about what they were doing.

However, Candice was under the impression that he fooled around and played women. There was a difference. Or at least *he* thought so. His mission wasn't to deceive a woman into thinking there was something more than the obvious going on, with the obvious being a great time in bed.

Then his thoughts went to Sophia and her comments about both of them shunning monogamy. Did he really feel that way? Joshua accused him of sleeping around because he didn't want a woman to have control over him like their mom had over their dad.

Her hand stoked his face.

"What's on your mind? You look so serious." Her voice was laced with sleep. "I'm sure something is troubling you because I know you can't be that into that kitty liter commercial."

He turned and saw her sleepy brown eyes looking back at him. "I'm sorry, I didn't mean to wake you."

"You didn't. I wasn't aiming for a full-on nap, I was simply dozing. The weather is so dreary and there was nothing good on TV." She wasn't going to let him sidestep the question, "What were you thinking about?"

"Trust me, you don't want to know. It's silly anyway."

"Let me be the judge of that; I like silly." She stretched and yawned loudly.

Landon laughed. "That must have been a good one."

"Yes." She said in the midst of more stretching. Candice sat up and patted the spot next to her. "Come sit with me. Why are you sitting on the floor anyway?"

He stood up and sat on the sofa. She moved to the other side of the sofa with her back against the arm and her feet stretched out resting against Landon's thigh.

"Family, work, or me?" She smiled at him expectantly.

"Huh?" He was puzzled.

"What's on your mind? It's either family issues, work or this mess you have gotten yourself into with me. So which is it?" She pushed his thigh with her foot to prod him to answer.

"Actually I was just sitting here thinking about all of the above; however I don't consider being here with you as 'a mess.'"

She smiled, "Spill it Phoenix. We have too many days to be together, so go ahead and get it off your chest now."

"I was thinking about the comment you made earlier. You indicated that I was some sort of ladies man."

"Uh huh? And?"

"And there is a difference in being in the company of women and stringing them along."

91

"'In the company of women?' What does that entail? Are you having tea, knitting, talking...having sex?"

"The later." He answered matter-of-factly.

"I see." She said and looked towards the television.

"I don't think you do Candice." She turned back to him. "There is nothing wrong with enjoying a purely physical relationship with a person as long as both parties know that's all it is."

"Just sex." Her voice was condescending.

"Basically, yes." He replied without remorse.

"And none of these women wanted to have a relationship with you?"

"Yes, some did, but I wasn't offering one and I made sure they knew that."

"How good of you?" She turned back to the television again and pulled her knees to her chest.

Landon took her reaction as if she was putting distance between them. She shunned him like he was wearing a scarlet letter.

"Candice look at me." She looked at him. "Everything is not always hearts and romance. Everyone doesn't want to be in a relationship where each party claims the other as their own. Sometimes it's just easier when there are no strings attached."

Candice was really trying to understand his reasoning. She looked at him in earnest.

"You've never wanted someone to call your own, a girlfriend?"

"No." *Not until now.*

"Why not?"

"Joshua says that I don't want a relationship because I want to prove to our father that a woman will never control me like our mom controls and dictates his life."

Neither of them said anything for several minutes. They looked at the screen, but were in their own private world. Landon wondered if what he'd confessed to her made any sense or did it make her re-think going away with him.

Candice new exactly how it felt to be controlled, and could actually understand Landon's behavior. She also felt sorry for him. Although she'd just gotten out of an abusive relationship, it didn't turn her against being in another with the right man. A man that treated her with respect, loved her and one who deserved to have her. It took her a long time to realize she was deserving of much more than she'd been given. Candice finally spoke.

"Do you feel that way? Is that why you don't want a relationship?" She stretched her legs out again.

"There may be some truth in what he says."

"What do you say Landon? Or am I being too nosey."

"You're worried about being too nosey now? You passed that benchmark ten questions ago." He smiled and those dazzling eyes left her speechless as they often did. She blinked and pretended to yawn again. "Am I boring you?"

"No. It's just been a long crazy morning. Are you going to answer my question?" She asked, not looking away this time.

"All my life I watched my dad do things he knew weren't right or that it would hurt Joshua especially, and yet he let my mom talk him into it. He always gave in to her. So, for a long time I've had in my mind that I would not be a man like my dad. I've gone out of my way to be as opposite of him as I could."

"You're not your father Landon. Don't let him keep you from experiencing something wonderful." He looked at her with a puzzled look on her face. "I've not experienced it either, but I know it's out there. Just look at Alexandra and Joshua."

"Yes, they do have a great relationship." He looked away from her. "It's hard to let something go that you've held on to for so long." She gave him a sad smile. He was tired of talking about his dad and said, "Well enough of that. What do you want to watch?"

"I don't know," she replied as she grabbed the guide on the end table. "Let's see." She brought it to his end of the sofa and they looked through the pages together.

How difficult will it be to let her go after only being with her for a short amount of time?

Chapter 9

What's Wrong With Me?

"Where's my luggage?" Candice asked Landon as she watched the last few abandoned pieces come around again.

"Well it's definitely not here. We've watched that old brown Samsonite come around at least three times."

"It can't *not* be here. What do you mean it's not here? What am I supposed to do without my luggage?"

"Candice, you're asking me like I'm the guy who loads the bags on the plane. Maybe it will be on the next flight. We aren't due to leave London for a couple of days anyway."

She looked pointedly at him and frowned. "But you work for this airline."

"Yes I do, but I fly the plane, I don't handle the luggage."

"But what am I supposed to do for clothes until then? I don't even have anything to sleep in." Landon didn't see a problem with that at all. Candice in his flat without clothes was a perfect situation to him.

Their night in the honeymoon suite was incased in a thick fog of sexual tension. They spent the day ordering room service and watching television—something neither ever had time to do. He couldn't help the slow smile that lifted the corners of his mouth when he thought of how she buried her head into his shoulder during most of the scary movie she insisted they watch.

"Oh you think this is funny Phoenix? Not everyone can live out of just one carryon. My luggage could be on its way to Australia." Landon couldn't understand how they could have missed three large pieces of hot pink luggage in the first place, but he knew it happened.

"Calm down Candice, British Airways is pretty good about keeping track of luggage. Let's go to the baggage claim office to track it down."

It turned out that Candice's luggage had not made the connecting flight when they changed planes in New York, but was placed on the next flight to Heathrow Airport. It wouldn't arrive until later that night and would most likely not be delivered until the morning.

It was raining hard when they finally pulled out of the parking garage; too hard to want to go shopping for night clothes. Landon told her that he kept extra toothbrushes and she could sleep in something of his.

"So you keep a stocked supply of toothbrushes do you?" She said looking at him.

"Yes ma'am I do."

"How convenient." She turned to look out the window at the architecture, not noticing the irritation on Landon's face.

He tried to lighten his voice as best as he could when he finally spoke, "Well actually it is. I travel so often and always seem to leave my toothbrush in the hotel so I keep plenty at home to restock."

"I see, but fortunately I stuck a few toiletries and other essentials in my computer case." The essentials she mentioned were just a change of underwear. She, however, had no change of clothes or anything to sleep in. Her mother had once told her to make sure to carry at least a change of underwear and a toothbrush with her when she flew.

Landon could tell she didn't believe him. She also probably wouldn't believe that she would be the first woman to ever spend the night at his place. Most of the women he saw were in other cities and the ones that weren't, ever got an invitation to his private life. To them, he was just a globetrotting pilot; handsome, charming and irresistible. None of the women he dated

98

or associated himself with, really knew him, except for Sophia. Sometimes they went months without speaking to one another, but Sophia knew the real Landon. He didn't know why, but he wanted Candice to know the real him too and not the guy people thought he was.

It was after ten by the time they finally arrived at Landon's flat. Candice was thankful he had covered parking, because it was still raining. She tried to picture the "flat" Landon mentioned as the place where he lived, knowing it was simply a British term for an apartment. The flats where Landon lived simply looked like a row of town homes with not much difference in the exterior as far as she could tell, except they seemed to sit way above the street level.

They parked in the small garage that accommodated his compact SUV but not much else. They were both tired from the long flight yet there was anticipation that hung over them like a cloud of electricity charged air. Neither spoke as they entered Landon's home.

There was a flight of stairs just inside the door.

"After you." Landon said as he directed her up the stairs. "There's another entrance on the other side of the garage which serves as the main entrance to my place."

The stairs were a bit steep and she wondered how she would have traversed them with her huge pieces of luggage had she had them. Landon, on the other hand, was thankful she still had on her coat. Even the concealed view of her backside had him rooted to his spot. Though he was indeed attracted to her, he knew his hesitation was more the fact that Candice, the woman who he had been dreaming of, thinking of, and torturing himself with wanting, was walking up to his private living space armed only with a laptop, toothbrush, and something small enough to fit in a briefcase.

Life for Landon is so very good right now.

She turned to look at him. "Aren't you coming?"

He smiled at her, which always seemed to steal a little of her breath and increased the beating of her heart, but the smile he directed at her was classic Landon. She gripped her bag and adjusted the weight of it on her shoulder hoping the movement would distract him from the involuntary movement her thighs made.

Heat shot from their juncture, so intense and hot that she had to grab on to the railing to steady herself. Too late, she realized her actions elicited an immediate response from Landon. Leaving his bag behind, a few quick steps and he was pressed behind her—hands gripping her waist. She trembled and cursed her body for betraying her.

"Candice are you ok? You're trembling." He quickly slid her bag from her shoulder and placed it on the step below. His hands felt so right on her. His voice, filled with such tender concern, lured her to him. She was exhausted, frustrated, and uncertain about everything; this trip, her life, and even the fact she may never see her luggage again. At that moment she wanted to give in, in that spot, she wanted that man to hold her, care for her, and just for that instant, she longed for him to love her.

Candice leaned into his chest. Automatically his arms swallowed up her waist. "Baby what's wrong?"

"Just tired I guess." She responded, not missing the term of endearment and not caring that he may use it on countless women. She pretended it was only for her.

"Are you sure it's just that? Are you feeling ok?" He turned her around to face him. He was on the step below her but they were nearly eye to eye. Candice pretended it was love she saw in his eyes, ignored the voices screaming in her head that this was a bad idea, and slowly placed her mouth on his in a series of feathery kisses.

There was no objection. In fact, his grip around her waist gave her a bit of encouragement. She ran her tongue along his bottom lip and the tiny moan escaping from his throat only fueled the inferno at the meeting of her thighs that started the entire episode. She slid her hands around his neck, captured his mouth as if she intended on keeping it, and made love to it with her tongue.

Slowly, at first, she mated with his tongue. He gave her complete autonomy over the kiss and she relished in the confidence it gave her. She wanted to experience passion so profound it left her breathless, sated, and satisfied. She wanted the assurance to know she could spark excitement in a man so much that he would fill his mind with her.

She wanted Landon Phoenix—needed him.

The kiss generated a desire in her so great she felt she would soon spontaneously combust.

Landon was beyond startled. The entire day they spent watching movies in Baton Rouge, his fingers ached to hold Candice like he was doing at that very moment, but wanting not to offend or frighten her, he had not. Guilt crept along his spine for losing control. Then he realized it had been she, not him, who initiated the kiss he was now sopping up greedily. Her kiss was like a lioness staking her prey. She toyed with his lips, giving him the illusion he was still in control of his senses and just like a lioness's prey, he soon realized she had complete control of his fate.

Even though his tongue matched hers stroke for stroke, as primitive as a feline dominates a zebra, she dominated whatever was taking place on his stairs.

At that moment Landon knew Candice had to command her own fate in order to feel whole again and if he had to be submissive to her will, then by all means he would let her pounce on him. Landon knew there was no way they would spend the next few days, not to mention the next three weeks together without them ending up in bed. The passion between them was too volatile.

Candice broke the kiss but lingered with her lips still touching his. She didn't break her hold around his neck nor did he break his hold around her waist. "I don't know what's wrong with me."

He had no idea what she meant because as far as he could tell, she was perfect. He kissed the corner of her mouth. She pulled away, looked at him, sighed, and pouted slightly.

"What's wrong with me?"

Before he could speak, she buried her face in his neck and licked the place where there was a slight *thump thump*. He groaned her name and gripped a handrail. This woman was literally making his legs wobbly.

"Everything feels just right to me," he said.

Breathing deeply, trying to steady her heart, she laid her head on his shoulder. The rapid beat from her chest was not the only thing out of control.

"Candice?"

She simply moved away, picked up her bag, and continued walking up the stairs, leaving Landon behind to stare up at her at a complete loss.

Chapter 10

Afraid

He found her at the window looking out at the rain. Although he had a feeling she was really looking through the rain instead of at it. He was so confused. Only moments before, she was alive, passionate, and daring. He didn't ever remember being so completely turned on by any woman. Landon wondered why she thought she'd done something wrong.

Was she looking for some sort of absolution? Did she not think she was free to act on her feelings?

It was still raining heavily, so hard the River Thames was not visible below. He loved looking out over the water. Every time he came up his stairs from the garage he appreciated his view. He thought of it as a living, breathing, and moving work of art. Today was no different, though instead of taking in the scenery outside of the window, it was the woman standing at the window who captured him.

Landon placed his bag against the wall and watched her watching the rain. His arms ached to hold her, but he was a patient man. He needed to find out what she thought was so wrong with her. He had an

105

idea, but he needed to hear it from her. Even if it was a phantom problem she needed to admit to it out loud, only then could he begin to show her how wrong she was.

"Candice?"

"Landon, even with the rain pounding against the glass, this is such a spectacular view."

"Yes, it is." He only saw *her*. He made no move to join her and she didn't turn towards him. He simply waited.

"If I had a view like this, I would never leave it."

"Then don't"

"The window is the entire length of your apartment."

They spoke at the same time so he was unsure if she heard his statement. Wow, he couldn't believe he'd just said that, but knew at that moment he really didn't want her to ever leave.

Still standing near the stairs next to his bag, he waited. A few minutes passed and he wondered if he should say something, then she spoke.

"I've never done anything like that before."

"No?"

"No." The innocence in her voice from that one word held him hostage. Nothing else mattered at the moment. Not the rain. Not the trip. Not the lost luggage. Not the new career opportunity that was imminent. Not the relationship he desperately wanted to repair with his dad. Nothing mattered at the moment but the sound of Candice's voice.

He couldn't help but ask, "Did you enjoy it?"

"Yes."

"So did I."

"You don't have to say that Landon." She still had her back to him. He took a step towards her. She scooted over a bit and turned her shoulder in as if she was afraid of him coming closer to her. He stopped. His heart beat fast.

"Are you afraid of me Candice?" He never would have thought he would need to ask her that, but her reaction told him she was shielding herself from something.

"No, Landon." Neither spoke. "I'm afraid of me." He still didn't move towards her. He wanted her to come to him. He needed her to know that she could.

"Why? Why do you think something is wrong with you?" She said nothing, her back still to him. "Candice?" Silence. "Candice, look at me." He tried to say it as gently as he could. She turned towards him. Her face was passive and the practiced smile made him sick to his stomach. He instinctively knew this was the

107

face she put on when she had to pretend everything was ok. When she had to pretend she wasn't hurting. This was the face he never wanted to see again.

To hell with waiting. He walked over to her and enfolded her into the safety of him. He rested his head on hers and whispered, "As long as I'm around, you don't have to be afraid of anything or anyone, not even of yourself." He hoped like hell she believed him. He finally felt her body relax against him.

He held her like that for a few more moments. Not wanting to let her go, but he knew she must be exhausted. He was about to show her upstairs to where she would be sleeping, when she placed her head on his shoulder and spoke. Her voice was paper-thin.

"I'm afraid of my reaction to you when I'm close to you. My mind is saying 'no, this can't happen,' but my body just reacts to the feelings I'm having. I've never felt so out of control before."

"That's what happens when two people are attracted to each other. You don't have to feel bad about it. It's a natural reaction."

"But I just can't go around kissing you when I feel like it!" She slowly looked up at him, creased her forehead, and then put her head back on his shoulder. "I feel like doing it all the time." Her words were barely audible.

"Is that right?" He slid his hand up the length of her spine. She nodded her head in affirmation like a kid after a good cry.

"You are very handsome Landon." She said it like that very fact was reason enough.

He'd heard those words all his life, but it was the first time it wasn't used as a compliment. It was almost like some sort of criticism. He smiled inwardly.

"And do you have the same reaction to all handsome men?" He smiled at her when she looked up at him and she couldn't help but giggle at the absurdity of her statement.

"Of course not."

"Then why me? Not that I'm complaining."

"Because you make me feel good. You make me feel alive….and a bit bold" She put her head down again. "Landon, you make me feel sexy and…"

He waited for her to finish, but when he felt she didn't plan on continuing he prodded her a bit.

"And what?"

Silence.

"And worthy."

He wanted to tell her she was all those things. Landon especially wanted her to know that it wasn't her who should be worried about being worthy but him. Instead, he asked, "Why are you fighting it?" She looked up at him.

"It's so complicated Landon. I'm a mess."

He loosened his arms took a small step back so she could look at him.

"The feelings you are having, Candice, are mutual. I am very attracted to you and there is absolutely nothing wrong with two consenting adults enjoying a physical relationship."

"We can't have an affair Landon; it's not right."

"Does it feel right when you are kissing me? Because it sure as hell feels right to me."

"Yes but…" He pulled her to him and gave her a quick kiss to any halt any objections she was about to make.

It took ever effort he could muster to make the kiss as chaste as possible.

"Fighting it is futile, my dear. When you are ready to surrender to the feelings plaguing us both, then together we can explore how far our passion will take us.

"I want you Candice Carwin, like I've never wanted any other woman, but I need the decision to take our relationship to another level to be yours. You will have complete autonomy of how far we stretch the boundaries over the next three weeks."

He wanted to say more. He wanted to tell her that at the end of three weeks there was no way he would be able to let her walk away from him and return things back to normal.

He wanted to tell her that he needed his *normal* to include her. Instead, he took her bag off her shoulder and said, "Come on, you must think I'm a horrible host. You haven't even put your bag down. Let me take you upstairs and show you the guest suite."

He directed her towards another set of stairs, whereas the ones from the garage were nothing special, the stairs that lead to the second floor of his flat were beautiful. It was almost as if they were floating in mid air; gorgeous dark planks with no handrails on either side, which seemed a bit scary to traverse.

"Wow, I was so impressed by your massive window and the possibility of the view, I didn't even notice these stairs. They are almost like a modern art exhibit we had in the gallery a few months ago. How do you go up and down with no handrails?"

"I guess I'm just used to them. Come on. I won't let you fall."

111

She walked ahead of him. He tried not to stare at her backside, but it was impossible. They made it to the top without incident, but he couldn't help but think of the kiss they'd shared on the entry stairs.

He showed her the guest room with its attached bath and where the linens were located. She didn't have much to say so he figured she needed some time alone.

"If you like, I will give you something to put on and you can rest a while. It was a long flight and the time difference will have you exhausted for a few days until you get used to it." He needed to clear his head, breathe some air that he didn't have to share with Candice.

"Ok, I would love a nice long bath and I guess I better call my parents and tell them I made it to London."

Landon grabbed a pair of pajamas his mom bought for him that he never had any use for and sat them on the bed. He looked around the room while Candice pulled out her toiletries and other "essentials" from her computer case. Two weeks ago, he would never have guessed that Candice would be sharing his home. So unaccustomed to having company he simply said what hosts traditionally tell their guests.

"Let me know if you need anything Candice."
She smiled. "I will call the airlines and see if I can get someone to deliver your luggage tonight. I have some phone calls to make so feel free to make yourself completely at home."

"Thanks Landon. It will be great if I can get my luggage tonight." She just stood there and looked at him. He realized she was waiting for him to leave. He turned and closed the door behind him.

Landon spoke through the door, "We'll talk about what we will eat after you have relaxed a bit, but the kitchen is stocked full of snacks."

"Ok. Thanks again Landon." She replied.

For some reason he couldn't move. He wanted to come up with something, anything that he could say to convince her that it was ok to feel good. It was ok to want to kiss him. It was more than ok to act on any of the feelings she was having, especially if it involved anything like what happened on the entry stairs. He wanted her to stop fighting herself and surrender to the pleasures that had been denied to her. He wanted her to surrender to the pleasures he was hell bent on giving her.

Chapter 11

The Perfect Wife

Devin Freedman sat in his car looking through the papers the man in the rumpled brown suit had just given him. He'd needed the information right away though it cost him way more than his depleting funds could afford, but he felt it was worth the sacrifice. Devin had never seen the man before. He spoke to him on the phone twice, once to tell him what he was looking for and once when Devin was given instructions on when and where to meet him to receive it. Both times, the man he knew only as Cricket had called him.

All he knew about Cricket was he was a private investigator one of his clients used from time to time when his law firm really needed to dig deep for evidence. Cricket didn't have an office or business cards. He wasn't that kind of investigator. He was the guy that always got the information he was after, but no one asked how he got it. You didn't call him; he called you. He was the guy that just showed up out of the shadows and knocked on the car window scaring the life out of you.

Devin's heart was still racing even after he saw Cricket drive away in an old beat up Oldsmobile that he hadn't seen drive up in the first place. The car also reminded Devin of the suit the man wore—old and beat up.

He knew it. There was no record anywhere of Candice being married. Did she think, just because the law said they weren't married, that she no longer belonged to him? He looked at the other hand-scrawled sheet of paper in the envelope. *Phoenix*!

The confrontation in the hotel with the man who claimed to be Candice's husband still played in his head. It was bad enough that his company suggested he relocate to the Houston office, because of the charges that had been filed against him. He was forced to stay in a hotel when he had business in town because Candice got the house in the divorce and too much of his money. Now she was making a fool of him by parading around a hotel like some two-dollar whore with some mixed-breed bastard with too much testosterone.

She belonged to him, always had. Devin remembered the first time he saw her. They both were guests at a wedding. The groom was a business associate of Devin's and Candice was with her parents who were friends of the bride's parents. The wedding

115

was located at Houmas House Plantation and Gardens right outside of Baton Rouge.

He was sure the venue was chosen because of the gardens. If he bothered to care about those things he had to admit the scenery was ideal for a wedding. Most people toured the plantation for the gardens, but the plantation house was a classic work of architecture, with its huge porch and storybook columns.

Devin imagined a porcelain woman sitting there sweltering in the oppressive heat and humidity; because the social stigmas and customs dictated she nearly suffocate under the bindings of a corset that was pulled so tight it left her precious white skin marked by its presence. She would be sitting on that porch sipping tea while her slave girl fanned her with robotic rhythms using a fan weaved of tall grass gathered just for that purpose.

He guessed if he really had to think about the venue and its relationship to marriage it would be quite ironic. It's very difficult see the plantation house, look around at the grounds and think of its place in history with the massive amounts of sugarcane it produced, and not think of slavery.

It wasn't as if he was cynical about marriage, on the contrary, he was twenty-eight years old and eager for marriage. He knew it was vital for business.

Marriage promotes stability and offers opportunities to be invited to more intimate gatherings where business deals were cinched while other husbands who were annoyed by their own wives could be enamored by his.

Devin needed a wife who was beautiful and the epitome of grace and elegance. A wife other men would want, yet a wife that would be so absorbed with him that no man could possibly have a chance. He needed a wife to dote on him, be good for business, and one who could be carefully controlled. Yes, controlled and compliant, but not outwardly robotic and submissive like the slave girl.

It was the end of August, still hot and humid but on that particular day he remembered there being a slight breeze to keep the humidity at bay. Most of the women wore summer dresses with lots of back and shoulders out. Of course you couldn't blame them; it was in fact still August in the South, but still he thought most were underdressed for the occasion. Character and clothes dictated to each other.

He remembered seeing the preacher swat at a bee. No one seemed concerned. The wedding was on the grounds of a huge garden. He followed the path of the bee and that's when he spotted her. Sitting near the front in an aisle seat was the profile and back of the woman he pictured at his side.

117

Her dress was tasteful, showing of just a hint of shoulder; her hair hung in waves down her back, shiny and black. Her legs were crossed at the thigh exposing her knee but not too much more. The legs he saw could stop a truck. *Very nice. Classy.*

Most people were using their programs to fan away the heat, but not her. It was as if it was beneath her to let the heat know it caused her any kind of discomfort. *Self-control. Yes.* He also noticed she didn't have on heels like many of the other women— smart considering the wedding and reception was in the grass. *If only the front of her matched the rest.* It didn't matter what her mind was like, she would be his marionette anyway. *His slave girl.* Instead of grass, the *fan* will be weaved with respect, loyalty, and obedience.

Devin watched the woman with the crossed legs. He wanted to see her reaction to the bride and groom reciting their vows. It was slight and he wouldn't have noticed if he hadn't been paying close attention, but he saw how she angled her head a bit before she closed her lids for a few seconds. Devin smiled to himself. He wondered how long it would take him to have her robotically fanning him, mentally yoked and bound to him. *Until death do us part.*

The vibration from Devin's pocket startled him. He pulled out the phone, looked at the number, smiled and answered.

"Tell me you have good news for me."

"Devin, I could lose my job for this."

"You're being paid well. Did you make sure her luggage was delayed?"

"Yea."

"And?"

"The address is in the system... Devin if they find out what I did, I could go to jail." The voice on the phone paused. "And if they find out I went into the computer and gave out confidential information...well that's a federal offense."

"It's not like it's something you haven't done before."

Another pause.

Devin heard the sound of a doorbell ringing in the background.

"I have to go. I'll text you the information."

The caller disconnected the call and a few moments later Devin's phone chirped to indicate an incoming text. He smiled, checked his briefcase for his passport and confirmation numbers, and drove the rental car towards the airport.

Chapter 12

Relaxed

Candice's body seemed to melt instantly as she eased into the hot foaming water. She closed her eyes and listened to the soft splash of the water as it settled itself after the invasion of her long limbs and tense torso. The warmth and gently sway of the water from her slight movements were eager to lull her to the oblivion of sleep she longed for, but instead she opened her eyes to take in her surroundings.

There was an array of bath items with lavender scents on the shelf near the tub. He told her to help herself, so she had. All of her body wash and other bath toiletries were in her luggage. The items in the guest bathroom weren't her brand but they all had the scent she used. She always bought lavender. Interesting, but she didn't ponder the coincidence, just soaked and enjoyed being enveloped by the decadence of the bath. Even her scalp seemed to relax. She leaned back and rested her head on the edge of the tub where there was a cushion just for that purpose.

Why was she so uptight? She knew why. The question is: What would she do about it?

The water felt good. Too good. Exhausted and frustrated, she continued to relax and after a while she was so tranquil her body bobbed a bit. She placed her feet on the opposite end of the tub to brace herself. The tub was huge, but her legs were long enough to touch the other end. Normally she wasn't able to stretch out completely in a standard-sized bathtub and appreciated Landon even more for having this impressive soaking tub. As a matter of fact, everything in the bathroom was impressive.

She lifted her head to look around a bit more then leaned her arm on the side of the tub and rested her chin on it, as she took in the entire room. The water slid off her arm and evaporated into a white rug that was the length of the tub. She remembered it being very comfortable when she stood on it just before she entered the water. It cushioned her feet and she appreciated the luxuriousness of it.

Everything was white. The towels were huge and fluffy. One was placed on the little table next to the tub to use when she got out. Candice couldn't wait to wrap one around her. The bathroom was sort of spa-like yet very woman's-boudoir-ish. There was a vanity with a simple bench and padded leather white cushion.

The shower was incased in glass. It looked as if a family of five could stand in it easily. There were shower sprays ready to blast from every direction, including a huge square rain showerhead hanging from the ceiling. She noticed there was a seat in the shower.

"I guess," she thought, "it could be used to prop a foot up to make it easier to shave legs."

Why would he... The thought refused to surface completely. She continued her perusal of the shower. There were also two handles on the only tiled wall, but not handles that would be for someone who would need assistance in the shower. They were more like grips. *What in the world?*

Candice dismissed the shower from her mind, eased herself fully into the tub again, leaned her head back and closed her eyes. She let the warmth of the water infuse itself into every crevice of her body.

Hold on. Something wasn't setting well with her. She opened her eyes again and looked around. She'd been in guest baths before and they usually were decorated neutrally or either to the specific taste of the people or person who resides in the home. This bathroom was specifically decorated for a woman including all the bells and whistles they considered necessities.

Candice was sure if she opened one of the drawers built into the double sink vanity, its contents would spew femininity. Jealousy, hot, sharp and surprising, pierced her abdomen. Her heart beat quickly and she could feel the tension ease up her spine and settle into her shoulders. Frustration followed the tension because there was no reason for it. She had no claim on Landon or anyone for that matter. How he chose to decorate his bathroom or prepare it for guests, should not be any of her concern.

Yet she was concerned. She liked Landon and had from the moment they met. This trip had done nothing but expose her attraction for him. Her feelings for him were still buried beneath piles of excuses that inundated her mind. She wanted so much to be free to enjoy the bubbly sensation she got when he was around her. She wanted to be free to indulge in the smoldering sensual need that nearly choked her when he touched her or simply just looked at her.

Those eyes, that wicked grin, his compassionate tone, the fingertips that burned paths of desire into her skin with even the most casual of touches, were weapons she knew she had to defend herself against. She knew he used the same artillery to get other women to succumb to him. Anyone could simply look around for proof that he took great care in completely submerging them in Phoenix Seduction—enough to leave them completely stupid of what was happening to them.

Although he seemed attracted to her and she had shamelessly expressed her attraction for him, Candice could not allow herself to be controlled by lust.

Tired of thinking for the moment and just plain tired, she sat up and reached towards the other end of the tub, let the stopper release some of the water, flipped the lever to replace the stopper and began to refill the tub with more hot steamy water. She added more bath foam and leaned back to rest her head on the cushion.

It was difficult, but Candice tried to squeeze out the image of Devin harshly suggesting she soak in a warm tub of water after he'd inflicted bruises that usually covered her entire back. After a moment the stresses and tediousness of the recent days overcame the awful thoughts and she soon drifted off to sleep.

Landon padded around the kitchen in bare feet. He couldn't focus on anything in his office so he headed downstairs, for what, he didn't know.

He opened the refrigerator and looked in without out really seeing anything. He could tell Clarice had done the marketing, because the fridge was stocked. He closed the refrigerator door, walked to the pantry, glanced inside, and instinctively reached for a bag of chips and pick up a bottle of beer off the shelf next to them.

It took two beers before he felt relaxed enough to focus on anything other than Candice and the fact that she was most likely naked only a floor above him. Dismissing the thought, he walked up the stairs to call his new potential business partner, Ethan.

"I'm sorry Landon, but the earliest I could arrange the meeting was on Friday afternoon. Two days from now. Our Boston office was all set to handle things stateside so we have to transfer all the documents and key participants to London."

"No worries, Ethan, I know that my schedule change has disrupted lots of plans that were scheduled well in advance. I will just tell my travel companion that we will have to postpone our London departure for a few days."

Landon closed his eyes as he said the last few words, hoping Candice would understand and not be freaked out by staying in his home for a few more days. "I'll foot the cost of the added expenses for delaying the deal. This couldn't be helped."

He talked to Ethan a few moments more before he hung up the phone. A fax was coming in. He placed it in the file with all the other information he and his lawyer had gone over with a fine tooth comb. Landon was getting tired of always being in the air. Jumping from bed to bed no longer held its former excitement. He was ready to settle down. Not saying that he was ready for the house with the picket fence, wife and kids just yet, but he was ready to store his suitcase for a while and not have to reset his watch every few days.

Landon still wasn't sure if partnering with Ethan was something he should do, even though they were going to finalize everything in only a couple of days. Everything looked great on paper, but his gut was telling him to make absolutely sure this guy could deliver what he's promising. Not only was it a huge financial risk, but if things didn't work out as planned a whole lot of people could lose their homes and livelihoods.

Landon heard the hum of the fax machine again and waited for the paper to roll out. He was waiting on a report from a background check he'd done on Ethan. He picked up the sheet.

"Landon."

Candice stood at the door of his office. He turned to face her. Good lord, why did he do that? Her hair was tied up in a towel and she had on the cream colored pajamas. The fabric clung to her damp breast and accentuated the fact that she wasn't wearing a bra.

126

"I'm sorry to disturb you Landon, but I wanted to let you know that I'm going to lie down for a little while. I'm really tired."

"You aren't disturbing me Candice. Did the bath help?"

"Yes, it was great. It is like a spa in there. My favorite scent and everything. You really know how to treat a lady don't you?"

"Well apparently my house keeper knows a thing or two, because the last time I looked in there it was completely empty except for the mainstays—you know, toilet, tub, shower. But I'm glad she made it comfortable for you."

"She did all that for only a couple of nights?"

"Yea, I guess so. She has been dying to decorate that bathroom so I guess when I said I would be having a female houseguest she went crazy."

"And speaking of the length of stay, I have an important business meeting on Friday. That is the earliest the stateside party can arrive. I'm sorry we will have to postpone the trip a couple of days."

"That's not a problem Landon; it will give me more time to do some sightseeing here in London. Wake me in a few hours if I'm not up before then."

"Ok." He watched her walk away. He smiled, two more days with Candice in his town. He turned back to the fax. Ethan Powers checked out clean, but there was still something tugging at him about the guy, like he was missing something that was right there.

Chapter 13

The Surrender

*Knock, knock, knock…*Landon wasn't sure if Candice was a light sleeper or not and he didn't want to startle her so he knocked lightly on the door. When she didn't say anything, he turned the knob; it was unlocked. He walked in and paused at the sight of her. She was lying on her side, her hair splayed out on the pillow. She looked so peaceful. He moved towards the bed wondering if he was about to scare the hell out of her.

"Candice."

Nothing…

"Candice."

She slept so soundly he questioned whether he should wake her or just let her sleep. She will be up all night if he didn't. He sat on the bed, still she did not stir. She's so beautiful he thought. With the back of his hand he stroked her cheek. He was sure this was bordering on creepy behavior.

"Candice."

She stirred and looked up at him.

"How long have you been sitting there?" she asked while pulling the covers over her head.

"Long enough to know you are a sound sleeper. You've been asleep all day. I figured I better wake and feed my house guest."

"I've been asleep a while?"

"Yes, now come on." He shook her by the shoulder to keep her from going back to sleep. "I know you're probably starving. How about a sandwich? And I can probably produce a glass of wine. I believe the rain has stopped. We may be able to see the lights from the boat houses."

She pulled the comforter from her head and looked at the window. It was dark outside. "Is it morning?"

"Nope it's just after 8PM."

"Urgh! My sleep will be all jacked up." He tilted his head and raised an eyebrow at the slang she used—this was new. His mouth tilted into a half smile to hear her speaking so casually.

"For a few days, yes. Come on. The glass of wine will help."

"Do you have any beer?"

He was just about to stand up when her question stopped him. He turned and looked at her in surprise. "You drink beer?"

130

"Yep! Is that a problem?" She smiled knowing he was trying to picture her tossing back a beer. Then apprehension coated her belly as she wondered if he had any hang-ups about what women should and should not drink.

"No problem. Beer will go great with my Phoenix Sandwich Surprise. Cold or room temperature?"

Relief washed away the apprehension. *Was it just Devin who felt that way?* She recalled he'd asked her a question and brought her thoughts back to Landon. "Room temperature?" She asked as she sat up awkwardly in the bed.

"Yes, that's how we drink them over here in the old country." He smiled and winked at her.

She pulled her knees to her chest. "I'll have to give it a try one of these days, but for now, I'll take a cold one if you have it."

"I do. It will be waiting on you when you come down. Take your time." He headed towards the bedroom door dressed in a pair of black lounge pants that hung low on his waist and a simple gray t-shirt. She couldn't see his feet. "I will check on your luggage in a bit." Candice nodded; waited until she was sure he was busy downstairs and then got up and headed

131

towards the bathroom. She at least needed to splash a bit of water on her face before she sat down for dinner.

Damn, she looks good in my pajamas. In my kitchen. In my house.

They cleaned the kitchen in silence, though every so often she looked up at him offering him an apologetic smile. For what exactly, he couldn't tell. He wanted to hold her in his arms and assure her there were no nightmares in the safety of them. Instead, he just stood watching her at the window wondering what was going on in that beautiful head of hers.

Landon turned off the lights in the living area so Candice could have a better view of the Thames coming alive under the night sky. He stood at the counter near the wine chiller and watched her stare out of the window as if she was seeing more than what was there. Maybe she was.

She hadn't talked much at dinner and not for lack of trying on his part. There were a few times he felt she wanted to tell him something, but when he pressed her she merely said the sandwich was delicious and asked for another beer.

The view was breathtaking—literally. He realized he was holding his breath as not to disturb the picture of her gazing out of his window.

The silk of the cream colored pajamas fit loosely on her, but her girl parts were definitely noticeable. Landon couldn't see himself wearing anything as formal as pajamas to bed, but oh how he wanted to follow the pattern of the thin black strips with his hand, from shoulder to ankle with her in them and out of them.

Just as he finally made up his mind to at least walk over to the window with her, his cell phone rang. He reached for it on the kitchen counter. He didn't recognize the number, but it was local.

"Yea?"

He answered, sounding more annoyed than he intended. Candice turned around with a hopeful look on her face, then surprise after she heard the annoyance in his voice. He felt like an idiot; he'd completely forgotten the airline would be calling him back. They'd been too busy to look when he called right before he and Candice sat to eat.

He placed the phone back on the counter and walked towards her near the window.

"They have your luggage. They will be delivered tonight.

"That's great. I was afraid I was stuck in these for the next three weeks." Indicating the pajamas she wore.

If he had anything to do with it, pajamas would be the last thing she covered her body with. He felt he could fit the bill perfectly.

"You don't like my pajamas?" He asked.

"Yes they are very nice, but my own clothes will do just fine."

"Yea, you don't seem to me to be the type for men's pajamas."

She turned towards him with a scowl on her face.

"So speaking of type, what is *your* type Mr. Phoenix? All body no brains? Someone who will be at your beck and call?"

He raised a brow; where did this attitude come from. He was beginning to wonder if she was a bit nuts. *What the hell…* His eyes were smoldering gray diamonds, but he remained motionless.

She continued speaking, "Or do you prefer a woman who is all business—show up, do a back flip or two, wipe off her fingerprints and ease out of the door before you can return from flushing the condom down the toilet?"

He leaned his shoulder into the wall near the counter.

"I really didn't think crass was your style." He replied.

She felt her cheeks burn and turned to look out the window again.

"It's not. I'm sorry. I don't know where that came from." He didn't move and neither did she. She saw what looked like a houseboat, lit with lots of twinkling lights and people briefly stepping onto the deck and then quickly ducking back inside from the cold. The rain had long since stopped, but the river rocked as if it were still restless from being disturbed from the deluge.

"I mean, you don't have a steady girlfriend and practically get insulted every time I've brought up the matter. So I figured you are picky to the point where no one fits your standards or you are just in it for the sex. When you're in it for the sex, amenities are avoided at all costs."

"Amenities?" He asked.

"Yes,… you know… like cuddling, bathing together, naked eggs, talking until dawn, eating from the same fork on one piece of pie, board games in bed,"

He straightened, wondering if she were going to face him.

She continued as if she was talking to the night. "…kissing just because you can't go another moment without feeling your mouth on hers…love."

135

The wall clock announced passing seconds with its *tick tick* cutting through the night like a like a stick slamming against her taunt nerves. She turned to face him again.

How could he say that his type was her?

She stood there staring at him, waiting for an answer.

"I like a woman who takes care of herself. Physically, I love legs, but it isn't a deal breaker.

She could feel herself stand a little taller. She'd always felt self-conscience of her legs but at that very moment she was grateful for them and resisted the urge to elongate them by pointing her toes.

Devin ridiculed her and made her feel gangly and awkward to be so tall, though it was her tall regal air that attracted her to him in the first place. She knew it intimidated him when she wore heels because she could look at him eye to eye. She had a closet full of flats for that reason. Consequently, since the divorce she wore stilettos as often as the situation allowed.

"Candice?"

"Yes?"

"Are you ok or am I boring you?"

"Yes."

"Which question are you answering?"

"I'm ok. What is a deal breaker?"

He looked at her intently. She seemed as if she was waiting for absolution or something.

"If I can't have an intelligent conversation with a person, that's a deal breaker. My *type* is quite the opposite of what you envision as the nature of woman whom I like to keep company with. Whomever you think I am, I am not that guy."

"I want a woman who tells me exactly what she wants so there are no misunderstandings—a woman who knows what *she* wants and is not afraid of getting it. I want a woman who isn't afraid to stand up to me, but doesn't mind being submissive at times."

He saw her cock an eye toward him, positioning herself in that stance that all women take when they are about to tell some man—any man, that she is not about to sit back quietly and pick up the crap he is putting down.

"Holster your guns Candice, I simply meant that I like a woman who gives as well as she gets."

She relaxed her stance, put her head down a bit and peeked at him through her lashes. He knew she was contrite. Landon reached in the wine cooler and grabbed a bottle of wine. He felt he had to do

137

something with his hands. Just standing was making him nervous and that feeling was quite unfamiliar.

"Wine?" He lifted two glasses in her direction and turned his back to her to begin to pour before she gave him an answer.

"No."

He nearly spilled wine on the counter. The voice he heard in response was no longer across the room. It was at his ear. The word hung heavily between them.

She was there, standing right next to him, no longer wearing a shawl of uncertainty. He could see it in her eyes, hear it in the single word that still echoed in his ears, and feel it in his pants where his manhood was responding with assurance, whereas he was at a total loss. Nevertheless, he could taste the sweet anticipation of something life altering.

"No wine?" He managed to ask, still not completely facing her.

"No." She breathed the word and it entered him, filled his lungs and he held it there and waited.

"No Landon, I don't want any wine."

He put the bottle down and turned towards her. He was afraid to speak, to exhale. He was afraid to break whatever spell that had taken over her, him—

them. But he had to say something. He could tell she was expecting a response.

Exhale (yes, men do it too).

"What *do* you want Candice?" He didn't recognize the voice as his own. It was low, raspy and seductive, yet apprehensively filled with anticipation, if that's even possible.

"You." Her answer was confident—sure.

"Ok." He didn't move. He couldn't. A thousand questions plagued him.

What would she do? Was she expecting him to make a move? Should he kiss her?

Her face had never been more beautiful to him, a deep rich brown, not a trace of makeup. Just as he brought his eyes to her lips, she gripped her bottom lip with her teeth and slowly released it. Their eyes met and seem to speak—no spoken word would have been adequate. He was vaguely aware that she was dressed in his pajamas. Her eyes left his and her head lowered a bit. He cupped her chin with his finger.

"Uh uh, don't leave me…What?

"Landon, I…" She looked directly into his eyes again. "Surrender."

No word ever carried so much weight with Landon. He knew that at that moment and all moments going forward, no other person would ever mean as

139

much to him as her. His Candice had surrendered. Though the battle was won, he knew the war was far from over. He hoped to God his heart was heavily armed.

Chapter 14

The Cliff

There, she'd said it. She'd admitted that she wanted him. Now what?

"Candice?"

Damn what does he want? For me to say, "Landon, take me now. I want to make love to you until I have trouble remembering my name?"

"Yes."

Her eyes widened. Surely he hadn't read her mind.

"Yes what, Landon?"

"Yes, tell me what was just running through your mind. I want to be absolutely sure I know what 'I surrender' means."

At first she thought about sidestepping the question with coy words about giving in to their attraction, but she decided to be honest with him and herself.

"I surrender to you, to us, to whatever it is that keep my lips seeking out yours for solace. I surrender to your arms, your caring, your kindness, your friendship and your insistence on us traveling

141

together." Her lips formed a half smile when she said the last bit to him and then it disappeared before she continued. "I surrender to your bed, Landon. I surrender to what I hope is your willingness to make love to me until I am senselessly grasping for the sheets and thoroughly spent." She stood as tall as her 5'9" frame allowed, looked directly into his smoldering pools and continued. "I surrender Landon to you, right now at this moment."

He couldn't say anything. What could he say? What was left to say? She'd said it all. And since there was nothing left to be said, he said nothing. Instead, he held her face in his hands, brought his lips to hers and greedily feasted on them. He parted them, dipped his tongue in her mouth and mated with hers. Her tongue was waiting to be captured and soon he found that he was the submissive one while she quickly controlled the tone of the kiss. Desire sliced through him like a machete. No words—action was in order. When air was necessary, he released her from his kiss and rested his forehead against hers.

"Here or upstairs?"

She knew what he was asking, but the kiss had stolen any form of coherent words. With the counter at her back she was fairly sure if her wobbly legs betrayed her she would at least have backup support.

Plus she knew London would not let her fall. Her trembling fingers found the top button of Landon's pajamas that she wore and removed the button from the hole that held it secure. Their breathing sounded loud to her ears.

She looked up into the eyes that were centimeters from hers and removed button after button until she was done. He simply looked into the eyes that were looking up at him. Her hands fell to her sides as if letting him know that he had it from there. He wasted no time.

Landon backed away just enough to scan her work. He slipped his hands underneath the top at her shoulders and with the slightest effort the garment lay at her feet.

"Even better than in my dreams." he said.

"Is that right?"

"Yes. Shhhh… In my dreams your mouth is too busy kissing me to talk."

"Is that ri—" She was about to ask again, but he held up his index finger to his lips. His playful smile she loved so much gave her another idea. Instead of protesting she quickly lifted his t-shirt over his head and began to place kisses on his torso.

Landon inhaled sharply. He could wait no longer. With her shirt already on the floor he had the mind to make love to her on the damn counter, but he quickly decided he'd better play it safe and let their first time be in the bed. Maybe in two hours or so, he would take her on the counter, though her kisses were driving him insane.

Candice began kissing Landon on his neck and sucked on his earlobe. That was nearly his undoing. After all he was only human. She grazed her teeth on his lobe and whispered, "I surrender Landon."

She wouldn't have to say it again.

The sharp squeal of surprise was the only sound that followed Candice's words. Landon scooped her up with ease and concentrated on taking the stairs as fast as he could climb them.

When he got to his bedroom he placed her topless on the bed parallel to the headboard. Since he was shirtless as well all that was needed was for him to get rid of the bottoms. She lifted herself onto her elbows to watch. He jerked his lounge pants down, quickly removed one leg at a time and tossed them. They landed on his dresser knocking over something but he did not care. There he was before her, naked and gorgeous. She'd never cared to look at Devin naked, but she couldn't take her eyes off of Landon.

"You look just as good out of clothes as you do in them." It seemed to be such a revelation to her that he paused a moment before going to his closet to retrieve a pack of condoms. He didn't have any in the nightstand because he never had anyone over.

"Do I now?"

"Yes," she said with earnest.

"Hold that thought." He took long quick strides to the closet and returned to her without breaking too much of the momentum.

"Your turn." He said it as he leaned over and slid off the pajama bottoms she was wearing.

She looked up at him expectantly.

"What?" He asked.

"What do you think of me?" Her tone was soft, almost shy.

He knew she wanted approval, acceptance, assurance, anything to let her know that he found her desirable.

"Oh Baby," he said with a tone of reassurance. "You are breathtaking, but I can show you better than I can tell you."

He slid into the huge bed next to her.

"Aren't you going to turn off the lights?" she asked.

Bless her heart, he thought.

"If you want to, I will, but I've wanted to see you, all of you, this way for quite some time now. You are so beautiful Candice. I want to see you." He brushed the back of his hand along her cheek. "But if it makes you uncomfortable, I will." He traced his fingers along her neck across her breast and down to her navel. She giggled and wiggled to get his fingers away from her ticklish area.

"It doesn't." She replied suppressing her giggle.

"Are you sure?"

"Yes."

He continued his tour of her body, not quite venturing towards the apex of her thighs. He gently caressed her with his fingertips—too gently. She squirmed under his touch. She was very ticklish and the light grazes across her skin was awaking all her sensitive spots. She was sure giggles were not the sounds he was going for.

"I won't break Landon. It's ok. You can touch me...I want you to."

Landon placed the palm of his hand flat on her stomach and ventured south. The giggles turned into a stuttered moan. He wanted that moan. He wanted to taste it on his tongue, feel it vibrate on his lips and hear it mixed with the hitches in her breathing. He kissed her slow at first, but the sounds of pleasure that radiated from her as he parted her folds with deft fingers, caused him to go nearly mad with desire.

She latched on to his tongue and sucked. His finger sought out her swollen nodule. One of her arms was penned under him but her free hand gripped his shoulder and then his back. She seemed to be searching for something; sure it was there but unsure exactly what she should be looking for.

Candice released Landon's tongue and moaned into his mouth. He pulled her bottom lip into his mouth, needing to breathe but not willing to let the kiss go completely. He could feel her moisture pool beneath his fingers and he was eager to taste the essence of her.

Moan's of protest only charged him more and sent him on a mission due south.

Every hair follicle tingled, every nerve was heightened and her heart raced wildly. What was this man doing to her? He'd only touched her for a few seconds.

And why, for the life of me, do I keep moaning like a two-dollar whore on a Saturday night?

Was sex supposed to feel this good? Never in her life had she felt as she did under the hands of Landon Phoenix. Candice thought she would die of shame when he began touching her between her thighs.

147

That feeling died quickly and was replaced with need. Need that she could not comprehend nevertheless explain. The kissing and the touching were building up to something that had been allusive until now. She could feel herself climbing up a mountain. Organs played loudly in her ears, like in the movies and everyone knows something exciting is about to happen. Then he stopped.

No…no…no.

What was he doing? Then she realized he was about to touch her again, but in a way she'd never been touched before.

Candice felt Landon part her thighs with his hands. She looked down at him and his eyes were as full of desire and need as she felt. She trusted him.

The moment she laid her head back against the bed she felt Landon kiss the inside of her thigh. Dear Lord. Something was happening down there because he moaned with delight.

The ceiling faded from sight when he took those same lips that he'd so masterfully kissed her mouth with and kissed her where his fingers had previously been. No one or nothing mattered to Candice but what Landon was doing to her at that very moment. She gripped the comforter and then found

148

she'd placed her hands on Landon's head as she moaned incoherently.

The organ played louder reaching a dramatic crescendo as she fell gloriously off the cliff.

"That, my dear, is the first of many. I hope you know what you asked for." Landon made the declaration as he kissed the inside of her thighs again.

He was trying to give her a moment. His need was too great to allow for more than that. He stood in front of her. She sat up on her elbows again and admired him like she was viewing a great work of art. Before he could move over to the night stand to grab a condom she sat up and placed her hands on his hips.

"Wait Landon, let me look at you?" She felt bold and adventurous. She looked up at him with innocent eyes, though innocent was far from what he felt. In fact, his thoughts and plans bordered on being down right scandalous.

"May I?"

"Yes." He didn't know what she was asking and damn sure didn't care. She had carte blanche with him. Her hands burned a path of desire right to his shaft. He ached to enter her. Just her tentative touch and curious eyes were pure torture. He gritted his teeth and closed his eyes.

What the hell was she doing to him?

He'd never wanted a woman as badly as he wanted Candice.

Candice kept one hand on his hip and moved the other to touch his swollen member. She brushed it lightly with her finger tips. There was a hitch in his breathing. She looked up at him and saw his closed eyes. It encouraged her. She enclosed her hand around him. Never had she been so bold. Never had she had an urge to touch a man so intimately.

Candice wasn't really sure if her curiosity was proper sex etiquette but she really didn't care. She was aching to touch him this way. He was magnificent. The skin there was darker than the rest of his body and she was fascinated by it. She closed her eyes and felt it. She figured it was the artist in her to want to feel the texture of him. The shaft felt so good beneath her fingers, smooth and silky. The skin was tight but shifted easily as if it wasn't attached. She squeezed it and experimented with the movement again. She was about to run her fingers over the head when she heard him moan loudly through gritted teeth.

"Candice Carwin, I'm not sure what you are aiming for but if you keep that up I can't be held responsible for the results. Baby, if you are into torture then you have succeeded."

She was surprised. She had no idea she'd had such an effect on him. The term of endearment did not go unnoticed ether. It made her feel like she belonged to him and for the first time in her life it felt good.

"I'm sorry Landon." She placed her hands in her lap and put her head down, but the wicked smile could not be suppressed.

"There is no need to be sorry. It's just that I want you so badly."

She smiled up at him, scooted back to the center of the bed and said, "Here I am. Want me no more."

His eyes shot silver sparks and his need was apparent. He smiled slowly.

"I have a feeling that I will never tire of wanting you Candice." He reached for the condom, tore off the wrapper, tossed it to the floor and slid it over himself. Candice smiled, parted her legs in welcome and waited.

He'd intended to lick, nibble, and kiss her chocolate skin before he entered her but that little fondling of hers made it impossible for him to wait. And that little welcome gesture was too much for him to handle. Instead, he wanted to hold her and bury himself into her. He wanted to feel her legs wrap around him.

Instead of sinking into her as he planned; he shook his head. She looked disappointed and instinctively slid her legs close.

"No?" she asked.

"No." he said as he reached for her hand, she took it and with one quick movement Landon pulled her to him and she found herself straddling him on the edge of the bed. He smiled, lifted her by her bottom and eased her onto him. He knew it would be quick but he would make up for that later. She grabbed his shoulders and pushed herself down onto him.

Landon buried his face into her breast and she rode him slowly.

"Candice, what spell have you cast on me?" She replied by riding him harder and faster. He pulled her down hard by her waist. "Candice!" His release was immediate and overwhelming. Landon wrapped his arms around Candice and squeezed her tightly, feeling as if she was an extension of him. He had experienced great orgasms before, but with Candice his entire body seemed to come apart and began putting itself back together... around her.

His heart beat a little differently. It felt bigger, fuller.

It scared him.

Landon held on to her as if she was a life line. Maybe she was. So he just held her there, naked with nothing between them, but the sound of their breathing.

He didn't know how to let go.

Chapter 15

Business Trip

"Mr. Phoenix, the itinerary is on your desk. I faxed the paperwork to Mr. Powers a half hour ago. Also, the files that you need are in the large envelope near your computer. The other files are in my laptop and backed up on your flash drive labeled 'Power's Deal.' The car service will be at your home in about four hours. I will meet you at the airport. Do you need anything else?" Gloria opened a drawer and pulled out her purse. "I'm going to run out to grab some lunch. Trina will be here, but she isn't as familiar with the Powers deal as I am so if you have any last minute questions, call. I'll be back as quickly as I can. I've been working on it on my own so I know that all the paperwork is—"

"Perfect?" He added, finishing her statement. "I don't even know why you have an assistant; you never let her do anything." Dixon Phoenix walked into his office with Gloria at his heels and spotted his lunch laid out on the little conference table he used for very private meetings and when he needed more space than his desk allowed.

"I was going to say, a bit confusing to someone who isn't familiar with my organization methods for this particular deal."

Dixon stopped at the table and stared.

"What's wrong, did you want something different?" Gloria asked indicating the lunch she'd arranged.

"Something different? You have enough food here for the entire staff."

"Well I wasn't sure what you wanted and I knew you wouldn't take the time to go out to grab something for yourself. So I picked up a few things from Jessie's Tavern."

"Always looking out for me. Gloria, you are the best." And he meant it. She took better care of him than his own wife. "What's in the container?" He pointed to a clear container with a blue top.

"Oh that's your dessert, carrot cake."

He smiled and picked it up.

"You made this?" He said lifting the lid and inhaling the sweet deliciousness of it.

"Put that down, you need to eat your lunch first. And yes, I made it."

He put it back on the table like an obedient child.

"Jessie's sells carrot cake. I get it all the time."

"Jessie's cake has too much sugar and you know you aren't supposed to have it. You think you've been getting theirs but you've actually been eating my sugar free version."

"Really?" His face registered the shock he felt. "How long have you been doing that?"

"Since the cake became a staple in your lunch order. You get it just about every day." She looked at the container on the table. "When I send my assistant to pick it up for you, I ask her to get a dessert container. I put mine in the container from Jessie's and you have never been the wiser. Until today." She rolled her eyes and sighed. "They forgot to put the container in the bag." She smiled guiltily up at him. "You've found me out."

Dixon stood there with an incredulous look on his face and then began to laugh. "Do you mean to tell me I could have been eating cake without the guilt?"

"Yep."

Gloria looked at her watch and back at Dixon. "I better get going so I can be back before your next appointment. Let Trina know when you are done so she can remove all of this," she waved her hand towards the table, "before Darla Jacobs shows for her interview with you."

Dixon had forgotten all about the interview he was supposed to give the Boston Herald about the opening of the new children's clinic his company funded. He quickly pushed that thought to the side.

"Why don't you join me for lunch? There is more than enough and it's the least I could do for the great trouble you have gone through."

Gloria fiddled with her clasp on her purse, adjusted her strap and looked at her watch again.

"Thanks for the offer Mr. Phoenix, but I also have an errand to run so I will be ready to leave for our trip this evening."

He didn't press her. He could tell she was trying to get out of the office as quickly as she could.

"Ok, I'll see you after your lunch then."

"Yes Sir, and like I said, I'll be back as soon as possible." She rushed out before he could say anything else.

Dixon picked up the container again. How often did she bake cakes for him? Why would she go through all that trouble in the first place? He sat at the table, put the container down and looked at all of the food placed there. Roast beef and Swiss on rye with one tomato and a hint of mustard, a bowl of clam chowder with a sprinkle of paprika on top, and a chicken pot pie. Normally he only chose one of entrees she laid out for him, though they were all his favorites.

He looked at the container of cake again. When did she have time to bake? She was usually at the office before he got there and would be there after he left on many occasions if he didn't make her leave. Every morning all the appointments and files were sitting neatly on his desk and even the minutest detail was taken care of.

He knew she wasn't married. Her husband passed away only a year or two after they'd been married and that was nearly twelve years ago. He didn't think she was dating, because she never mentioned anything to him about it and when he brought up the matter she brushed him off as if it was the most ridiculous thing he could say.

She definitely was a great catch. Dixon spotted many clients and staff members flirting with her and asking her out. She never budged or at least he didn't think she did. Even some of the young interns found a reason to visit her desk and developed mild infatuations with Gloria.

She was very efficient at her job, but he had to have been blind not to notice how stunning she was. Always professionally dressed, nothing too tight or revealing, but she had a great figure for any age—

especially for a woman of fifty-five. Her facial bones
were delicately carved, her lips full. She had flawless
light brown skin and her green eyes were curiously
striking, though if Dixon had to pick her signature
feature, it would be the soft mass of curly black hair
that framed her face.

He knew that many African-American women
were beginning to wear their hair in its natural state,
but he also felt that some of the styles were a bit
eccentric for his taste. Gloria's hair fit her and he'd
found himself wondering on many occasions what the
texture of it would feel like. He was fascinated by it
and wanted to touch it like a kid who is curious with
hair unlike their own.

Any wife would be envious for their husband
being in contact with such a beauty all day. In fact he
had the feeling that it was the reason Gloria left her last
job. However, Jocelyn thought the woman was so far
beneath her that she barely gave her a second glance,
ironic, because Jocelyn could never measure up to
Gloria.

The only thing Jocelyn cared about was social
status. She'd never baked a cake for him in his life, or
even considered what kind of cake he would like.

Dixon tried to put thoughts of Gloria out of his
head but found it nearly impossible as he looked down

at his lunch knowing that she took the time to hand select it all to his specific tastes.

His cell phone rang, breaking him from his musings. The caller ID indicated it was his wife, Jocelyn. He took a deep breath and answered.

"Yes, Jocelyn." He was glad he would be leaving on a business trip later that evening. He purposely scheduled his business trip to coincide with the opening of the clinic. Jocelyn often traveled with him—to show stability and strength in their company. He knew, however, she wouldn't think of leaving with so many upcoming opportunities to be in the press. She'd given him holy hell when she found out he was going out of the country.

"People are starting to talk Dixon."

He rolled his eyes up to the ceiling. "About?"

"You haven't shown up to any functions." She said it as if that statement alone was explanation enough.

"And?"
Dixon picked up the sandwich and took a bite.

"You missed the Christmas Ball, the BGOL benefit and the day after the clinic fundraiser, Arthur Hopkins saw you at the club having drinks at the bar."

"Do you have a point in there somewhere?"

"Dixon your sarcasm is becoming quite exhausting and your defiance is getting old. When did you stop being considerate?"

"I've stopped doing a lot of things and do you even know what considerate means?"

"People don't believe you've been sick." She totally ignored his question.

"Why would they think that in the first place?"

"I had to tell them something to explain your absences. So when Arthur told Shelia you were at the club she brought it up at lunch. I just know people are beginning to talk about our marriage. So if you miss the opening of a clinic *that's named after us*, the gossip will only get worse."

Dixon placed the sandwich back in the container, watched Trina walk to Gloria's desk, rifle through some papers, pick one up and walk back to her own desk. He shook his head knowing Gloria will notice the disturbance in her orderly workspace and give Trina a lecture about organization, office protocol, and whatever transgression Gloria feels she violated.

"Dixon are you listening to me?"

"When will you get it through your head that I no longer give a damn what you or any of those people think? They are not your friends Jocelyn."

161

"Arty and Shelia have been our friends for more than thirty-five years. Shelia's and my father were business partners."

"And if you lost all your money tomorrow they wouldn't piss on you if you were on fire. Or at the very least take you in and help you get back on your feet."

"I wouldn't dare show up on their doorstep penniless. How embarrassing that would be for them!"

"God help you Jocelyn."

Dixon disconnected the line. He couldn't wait to have an ocean separating him from his wife. He also hoped that somehow he would be able to spend some time with Landon, though it was very likely that Landon would be working.

Reaching for the sandwich again, he spotted the blue-topped container from the corner of his eye. What will it be like to be with Gloria away from the office? Dixon knew he needed her to keep the paperwork organized and to take care of some details that required more finesse than he could muster, but the prospect of traveling across the Atlantic with her gave him a twinge of excitement.

He sat the sandwich, picked up the container and popped the top off of it. It tasted a little sweeter, pleased his tongue just a little bit more knowing Gloria had baked it just for him.

162

Chapter 16

Good Morning

The light streaming in through the window announced to her it was some time in the morning. With her fine eye for detail, it embarrassed Candice a bit to know that she hadn't taken time out to take a good look at her surroundings. It was in her nature to appreciate the aesthetics but all she saw the past few days was Landon. He was very aesthetically pleasing to the eye, touch, *tongue*…, smell, and her ears couldn't get enough of hearing the care and desire in his voice. Candice's cheeks heated when she paused to think about his tongue on her and following his lead, her tongue on him.

Candice closed her eyes slowly, took a deep breath, opened her eyes and tried to refocus on Landon's room instead of the man. It seemed larger than she initially gauged it to be. There was a little sitting area near a window. She couldn't remember, but he must have the corner "flat." The bed was on the same wall as the entrance to the bedroom, leaving the wall that faced the Thames to be made completely of glass. Heavy black remote controlled curtains either let

163

the river in or provided privacy, necessary, because the
bedroom was essentially only two floors above the
busy river.

If the view wasn't stunning enough, the rest of
the room left nothing more to be desired as far as décor
was concerned. It was a delicate blend of masculinity
and whimsical design. The walls and ceiling were
painted a rich brown and covered with old silent movie
posters. Somehow the space fit Landon's personality.

There was even what looked like an old
projector in the corner next to a painted silhouette of
Charlie Chaplin. The furniture was bold and pretty
much works of art on its own. The massive king sized
bed was very welcoming and sturdy; *thank goodness*.
The headboard and footboard was covered in rich
black leather with a beautiful wood trim. She did
remember seeing its clawed feet. It was a monster of a
bed. Very masculine, very Landon—she had never felt
so safe and comfortable.

The gigantic soft yellow rug with a beautiful
black design she wanted to get a closer look at, seemed
to bring the room all together. With the black curtains
and movie décor, it was easy to pretend she was in a
movie theater. But for now, she didn't have to pretend
she was in bed with Landon.

She felt him stir.

"Shouldn't they have been here with my luggage by now?" Candice asked Landon as she snuggled her back into his front. She didn't have to worry about jetlag keeping her up all night. Landon kept her busy enough as they passed the sleepless hours. And boy oh boy did he know how to pass the time.

Landon held her tightly against him. She could feel him getting aroused again. It made her feel powerful and sexy, knowing she could still command such attention from the power he wielded between his legs. *Mercy!*

"The luggage isn't being delivered here. Plus what do you need clothes for? I don't mind if you walk around wearing nothing at all."

She pulled away and turned to face him.

"Yea, I'm sure you wouldn't mind if I walk around here naked, but I prefer clothes when I go out. It is London, and winter at that. And what do you mean the luggage isn't being delivered here?"

"I had it delivered to a hotel in the area."

Candice sat up on one elbow. She stared at him baffled.

"Do you want me to leave?" Her heart beat quickly.

Landon brushed the back of his hand across her cheek. "How could you possibly think I would want you to leave after the night we had?"

"Well why is my luggage being sent to a hotel?" She tried not to sound like a spoiled kid but she was failing miserably.

He sat up with his back against the headboard and pulled her to him so her head would be resting on his chest. "I'm a very private person Candice. You are the only woman I've ever brought to my home. The fact is, there are a few women who are dying to find out where I live, I put the hotel address there just as a precaution. I don't want you to leave baby. I have to go out for a bit this morning and I will get it then."

She relaxed. It made sense though she couldn't keep the ache of jealousy from filling up in her stomach. The reality was that other women wanted Landon, so much so that he has to take *special precautions* to keep them away from his home.

What did he think they would do if they knew where he lived?

She wasn't sure she wanted to know the answer to that question so she decided to change the subject.

"What's with the silent movie posters and memorabilia?" She asked instead.

"Isn't it obvious?"

"Not to me?"

Landon reached over to his night stand and picked up a remote. What was he doing she thought. She really needed to get up to pee and brush her teeth. Her hair could probably use a good brushing too.

"Whatever you are about to do, hold that thought. I gotta pee!"

He laughed a little while she fished wildly underneath the covers near the foot of the bed. She pulled out the pajama top, slipped it on and fished some more. He took his left foot and slid it to the edge of the bed, dropping the sought-after pajama bottoms. Candice caught his sly movements and tossed one of the decorative pillows that had managed to stay on the bed, at him. He caught it, flung it to the side and headed towards her for retaliation. She squealed and jumped out of bed with just the pajama top on and quickly made her way towards his bathroom. She'd planned on scooping up the bottoms on her way but they were too close to the bed and Landon, who was waiting for her to get closer to him so he could pull her back into the bed. She decided against it, pulled the top down to make sure it covered her bottom and headed into the bathroom.

"There's no need in covering it Candice; I've seen every last inch of your pretty brown ass." He called after her. He also added, "Help yourself to whatever you need in there."

"Thanks Landon," she said through the bathroom door. "I think I will take a bath, do you have a t-shirt or something in here that I can put on?"

"There you go with the clothes again."

"Landon!"

"Yes, yes, they're on the middle shelf of the closet. Do you see them?"

Candice looked into the closet and spotted the t-shirts. "Yes. I'll be quick."

"Take your time."

Landon heard the water run in the tub and a few moments later he heard her get into it. That was the sound he'd been waiting for. He got out of the bed, walked to the bathroom door, turned the knob and was relieved it didn't stop, but turned all the way. He opened the door slowly.

She was neck deep in bubbles with her eyes closed. He eased in further so he could close the door behind him. She bent one of her legs and the wet knee and partial thigh view pulled him to the tub.

"What took you so long?" she asked, her eyes still closed.

He paused and smiled. She'd set him up. "Oh were you expecting me?"

"Yes. Why do you think I left the door unlocked?" She opened her eyes and tried to keep her tone even and not give away how startled she was to see him standing at the foot of the huge tub, naked with his arousal very apparent.

"I thought maybe you left it unlocked in case you needed me to find or give something to you."

She raised her eyebrows with an expectant look on her face. "And do you have something to give me?"

"Yes." His voice was low and sure. It dripped with unspoken promises.

She pretended to look for something in his empty hands.

"Well, where is it?" She asked as she slid her hand along her exposed leg. "I want it."

"Well then, my dear, you shall have it." Landon slowly eased himself into the warm foamy water and set out to give her a bath she would never forget.

Chapter 17

Charlie Chaplin

"How could getting clean feel so dirty?" Candice asked Landon as they snuggled in the bed again.

"It's all in the technique."

"Oh, so there is a technique to it?"

"Of course there is." He said it as he smiled and stroked her cheek with the back of his hand. The gesture of stroking her cheek was becoming a habit.

"And what is the technique?" She sat back away from him so she could look at him fully, though she loved when he touched her so tenderly.

Landon reached for Candice, pulled her and returned her to the spot she'd just pulled away from. She came back willingly; lying against his bare chest as he sat with his back against the headboard. "The technique is all in the placement of the bubbles." He smiled down at her and she pinched his forearm for teasing her.

"So now you can tell me about your décor." She said, getting back to their conversation before the bath that was more than a bath. She didn't even know people could have sex in the tub. She'd planned on washing all the towels they used to clean up the floor afterward, before his cleaning lady returned. There was no need for her to wonder why so many towels were used in such a short amount of time.

Talking about how his room was decorated was the last thing Landon wanted to do, but he figured her artistic eye wouldn't let it go.

"I didn't decorate it myself, if that's what you are asking."

"No, though I wondered, I was asking what was your inspiration for it."

"Oh, that's simple; I love silent movies. The entire era was classic Hollywood. And the blend of music and film was brilliant."

"There's still music in the movies now Landon, it's what sets the tone of the scene." Candice absently circled a birthmark on the inside of Landon's arm oblivious to the effect her touch had on him.

She looked up at him when he didn't reply. His eyes were closed. "Are you still sleepy?" she asked.

"No, just enjoying you touching me. Do you see what kind of effect you have on me?" She followed his eyes to see the sheet covering a very erect Landon. Quickly she moved her hand away from his arm.

171

Landon groaned, gathered her more tightly in his arms and threw a leg across her, pinning her to him.

"Do you see what kind of power you have over my body?"

Silence.

"I don't want to have power over you, Landon." Her tone was low and serious.

"You can't help it sometimes Candice, but as long as you use your powers for good, then everyone is happy." He tried to lighten the mood by adding, "I mean, when I start selling my furniture just so I can get to you and have you make little circles on my arm, *then* we have a problem."

She giggled, but decided to keep her hands to herself for the time being. "Like I was saying, there's still music in the movies now. It's essential to set the tone."

"I see what you are saying but the difference in a silent movie is that the music did more than set the tone; it spoke for the actors and gave sound to their emotions."

"I guess I've never thought of it that way. Do you watch them often? Who did the silhouette of Chaplin?"

"The decorator had a local artist do it and no, I'm not home often but sometimes when I'm trying to adjust to the time again, I get to watch them for hours."

"The artist did a good job at capturing the essence of Chaplin."

"Yea, Chaplin is one of my favorites. Most people thought he was an idiot, but he was brilliant and quite profound. Did you know he wrote, directed, produced, edited, scored, and starred in most of his films? He was so much more than the Tramp character he portrayed."

"No. I really don't know anything about him." Sitting up a bit, Candice looked around the room. She didn't see a television nor did she remember seeing one downstairs.

"Where do you watch TV? I haven't spotted one yet."

Landon reached for the remote, pushed a button and the small opening in the heavy black curtains closed. He pushed another button and a screen appeared from the ceiling. *His bedroom really is a movie theater.* She hadn't noticed the projector hanging from the ceiling, it blended in so well. Landon turned the lights off with another push of the button and she found herself in a movie theater atmosphere from the comfort of the bed.

173

"All we need is popcorn," she exclaimed in awe.

"That can be arranged." Landon replied with a playful smile.

"You sure know how to treat a girl, huh?"

"The only girl I'm concerned with is the one in my arms." And he meant it.

Landon's cell phone rang. It was Ethan. "I'm sorry Candice but I need to take this in my office." She watched him slide out of bed. She tried not to look at him walk naked across the room to his closet, but hell, she was an artist and far be it for an artist to not check out a great work of art when it's literally standing in front of them.

Again, Candice became acutely aware that she still did not have her luggage. She scurried into Landon's closet, grabbed a t-shirt and a pair of his lounge pants and put them on. She still felt naked with no undergarments on but at least she was covered. Deciding to give Alex a call and update her on what was going on, she went to the guest room to get her phone.

"Hello?" The word was spoken as a question and mingled with a yawn. It was a sleepy Alexandra. *Dear Lord she forgot about the time difference.*

"I'm so sorry; I forgot there is a time difference. I'll call you back later." The words spilled out almost at one time.

"Candice? What's wrong?" Candice could hear Alex moving around as if she was trying to sit up. "Is everything ok?" Joshua must have asked Alex who was on the phone because she heard her whisper, "It's Candice."

"Yes Alex, it's me. Look I didn't mean to wake the two of you. Go back to sleep; I will call you in a few hours."

"It's ok; where are you?"

"I'm in London." She felt awful for waking up her friend but knew she may as well answer her questions because there was no getting off the phone now.

"When are you leaving to begin the vacation?"

"To me this *is* part of my vacation. I guess I needed the time to get acclimated to the time before I could really enjoy being in Europe."

"How long will you be in London and how are things going with Landon?"

"We will be here through Friday because Landon has a business meeting he can't get out of and to answer your other question, Landon is a great host." She wasn't sure how much she should share with her friend because she still wasn't sure what was happening between her and Landon.

"So what have you done so far?"

There was a pause so Alex repeated her question. "I asked, what have you done so far since you've been in London?" *Oh the things she'd done so far, hell she still couldn't believe them.* Candice figured she'd better answer.

"Not too much, the airline lost my luggage. They've found it though. It was raining too hard when we got in yesterday to go out shopping so I've just been walking around in Landon's pajamas." She wasn't really sure why she called Alex, because it was making her feel as if she was lying to her friend.

"What's wrong Candice? You sound like you have something on your mind."

She knew she had to throw Alex a bone otherwise she wouldn't let up.

"I saw Devin the morning before we left."

"What happened?" Alex's tone changed instantly from detective mode to motherly. "Was Landon with you? That bastard! Did he say anything to you? Candice what *happened*?

"Well if you give me a chance, I will tell you."

"Sorry. I just know what you went through to get away from him and to know that you ran into him just ma—" Alex stopped talking abruptly and whispered in the background "No, she's ok. She's with Landon at his place." She came back on the line, "That was Joshua asking if you were ok...Tell me what happened."

Candice told Alex about the incident at the hotel without further interruption. She reassured her that she was fine and was glad she was getting away for a few weeks.

Until death do us part.

Devin's words rang in Candice's ears and a tear slipped out of the corner of her eye before she could catch it. Will she ever be rid of him and the demons that have shadowed her for years?

Chapter 18

DO NOT EQUATE SEX TO LOVE!
(The #1 rule in the *Falling in Love* handbook and also the #1 rule that is usually ignored.)

TV and books depict romantic over the top marriage proposals. Or at the very least, the man on bended knee proposal, but the truth is that the majority of proposals are made right before, during or right after some thumb-sucking-toe-curling sex. Period.

Great sex does not equal love!

Landon knew many men who had fallen victim to the aforementioned rule and he and felt sorry for the disillusioned blokes.

Landon played the rule in his head over and over. And over and over he remembered how he felt the moment their bodies joined as one. He felt like a traveler who had finally made it home. Candice was his home.

He no longer felt as if he needed to prove that no woman would control him like his mom controlled his dad. He felt finally at peace. He was willing to surrender whatever he had to her. He wanted to protect her, to love her, to make her part of his world where she was there every day when he woke and every night before he went to sleep.

Landon knew. The decision was made. He would give up his love of flying commercial airplanes, partner with Ethan Powers and fight like hell to keep Candice and make a home for them somewhere.

The rule played in his head again. He ignored it. It didn't apply to him. He was a goner the moment they'd met in Boston.

Landon walked to his closet feeling happy. Truly happy. The phone call from Ethan couldn't have come at a better moment. He would go meet with him at his London office, stop by the hotel to pick up Candice's luggage and then take her shopping and then to some art galleries he knew she would like. Landon reached for a pair of charcoal gray slacks and a white dress shirt.

The sound of his cell phone interrupted the tune he was humming. It was Joshua.

"Hello Baby Brother. You're up kinda early aren't you? It's just half past eight here and Bermuda is three hours behind so either someone is sick, dead, or your wife has you calling to get the scoop on Candice." Landon hung his clothes on the back of the bathroom door. "So…which is it?"

"Good morning to you too, Landon." Joshua replied. "For your information no one is sick or dead, thank goodness and my wife does not summon me to do deeds that you know good and well she would do herself."

"Touché… Well? It has to be something Joshua. It's 5:30 in the morning where you are. So what is it?"

"Alex is on the phone with Candice. She's telling her about Devin at the hotel where you two were staying. I know that Candice doesn't like to worry Alex so I'm calling to find out what *really* went down."

"I took care of it Joshua. No need to worry."

"Knowing that there was something for you to take care of, worries me. I've dealt with this guy Landon. Whatever happened, he's not going to let it go. He feels like he has a score to settle with me so if you gave him hell too…"

"I told the guy to stay away from my wife and if he didn't, he would be sorry."

"Excuse me? Your wife?"

"Long story, but I made the guy think Candice was my wife just to let him know that she no longer belonged to him."

"And he backed off?"

"He had no choice. Look man, I got this. I'm going to take care of her. That guy is done hurting her."

Silence.

Landon looked at his phone to check the connection. "Josh man, you there?"

Joshua cleared his throat and spoke in a softer tone.

"Have you told her?"

"No, she doesn't know I spoke to him." Landon reached into the closet to pull out a pair of shoes and rifled through his sock drawer for a pair of gray socks.

"Naw man. Have you told her you're in love with her?"

Landon paused, thought about denying it for a moment but realized he'd done enough of lying to himself. "No."

"What are you waiting on Man?"

"Josh, you know firsthand what that bastard put Candice through. That encounter with him in Baton Rouge really shook her up. She needs peace. I don't want to lay anything heavy on her right now."

"That's chicken shit and you know it Landon."

"Whatever Joshua. Candice is fine. We will be leaving on our trip Saturday. She is in good hands. End of story." Landon walked back into his bedroom, went to the door and peeked out to see if Candice was still in the guest room. He heard her talking on the phone so he went back to the bathroom to be out of earshot from her. The phone line was quiet again. Landon rubbed his hand through his short cut and realized he needed to get a haircut while he was out.

Joshua finally spoke again. "What about *her* story, Landon? What about the story you are denying her by refusing to be honest about your feelings."

Landon walked back into his bedroom, closed the door and sank in one of his chairs in the corner of his room. "What am I supposed to do, Joshua? What if the prospect of being with me scares the hell out of her?"

"What if it doesn't?"

What if it doesn't? Why is the worst case scenario always easier to believe than the possibility of the best case scenario?

"I'm scared, Bro." Admitting it was scary.

"Then you know that it's really love and not some need to be her hero. Love is scary, but it can also be the best thing that can happen to you."

"She is the best thing that has ever happened to me."

"Landon I don't have to tell you what an idiot I was when I met Alexandra. You were the one who

182

pointed out the fact that I let her leave without declaring my love for her. I almost lost her man. You gotta tell that woman how you feel."

"I hear ya Josh."

"I hope so Landon." Joshua paused for a couple of seconds then changed the subject. "By the way have you talked to the folks lately?"

"No, I'd planned on going by there this week because I had some business in Boston, but this thing here with Candice kinda sidetracked me."

"Well I received a call from Jordan Hayes…Do you remember him?"

"Tall guy with the stuck up wife…works at Lewis and Lewis?"

Joshua laughed knowing Landon knew exactly who Jordan and the stuck up wife were, especially since Jordan had walked in on Landon having extracurricular activities with her in her college dorm room two months before they were due to get married.

"Yea that's him."

"What did he want?"

"He asked if Dad was doing any better and if there was anything he and Jessica could do."

Landon frowned. "What's that supposed to mean?"

"I don't know but I haven't been able to get in touch with Mom or Dad to find out. Jordan also said Mom has been to the last few functions he's attended, alone."

"Dad wasn't with her?" His tone was filled with surprise and a bit of awe. Deep down he hoped that his dad was snubbing the functions to make a statement that his wife no longer called the shots.

"Nope."

"Well, keep trying to call them and let me know. I will be busy handling the situation on my end."

Landon stood and walked towards the guest room knowing for sure that Rule #1 did not apply to him, because he was scared as hell of how Candice would respond to his revelation.

Chapter 19

Releasing Demons

"What's wrong?" *Where had he come from?* Landon looked at the phone she'd placed on the nightstand. She looked up at him but did not reply.

He was dressed in a pair of slacks and starched white dress shirt.

When did he get dressed?

What *was* wrong with her?

She'd just told Alex about the awful things Devin said to her, but she was no longer upset to the point of crying.

"I'm ok." She stood and gave him a forced smile.

That didn't help.

His frown deepened.

She looked at his outfit again and asked, "Are you headed out?" He walked into the room, stood in front of her, but made no other move.

Hold me! Hold me! Hold me! She screamed on the inside.

"Talk to me," he said as he used the pad of his thumb to wipe another tear threatening to spill over.

185

Her mind was scrambling to come up with an answer for him but she just stood, unable to answer him.

"Come with me," he said as he took her by the hand and led her down the stairs.

Not wanting her to think what he had to say had anything to do with their bedroom activities, he figured the best place to talk was in the living area.

Candice followed behind Landon, holding his hand. She wondered if the hand holding was a romantic gesture or was he worried about her falling off of his stairs and breaking her neck.

She looked around and it was as if seeing his place for the first time. Whereas his bedroom was cozy and whimsical, his living area was done in a minimalist style. The furniture was sparse; there were clean lines and few accents. Landon led her to a cream colored leather sofa. It was much more comfortable than it looked. He sat near the arm and she sat beside him, turned towards him a little with their knees nearly touching. The heat clicked on, but she didn't need it because the heat between them was quite apparent.

Candice wondered what he expected her to say.

"Why were you crying Candice?"

"I don't know. I just felt overwhelmed all of a sudden." She looked up and his eyes were so spectacularly clear and piercing. But not in a bad way; they were the eyes she'd seen in her dreams.

What was it, she wondered, about eyes that told so much about a person? She could get lost in his eyes.

"What has you overwhelmed...me?"

"No Landon, not you...Well yes you, but.."

"But what?"

"I like being overwhelmed by you." She looked down at her hands again, and then pretended to pick some lint off of the lounge pants she wore.

"I'm glad." He reached for one of her hands and gently tugged on it. She looked up at him. "Talk to me Candice."

She tilted her head and gave him a sad smile.

"What do you want to know?"

"Come here." He pulled her to him so he could hold her. "I want to know why you are so sad sometimes."

"It's this Landon."

"What do you mean?"

"This... us sitting here like this together. You reaching for my hand, stroking my cheek...you holding me like this." He began to release her, but she stopped him and held his arm in place. "No. Don't."

"I don't understand Candice. I thought we were enjoying each other."

"That's just it Landon. I love being with you like this. Even if it is only for the moment, I feel safe. Wanted."

Landon held her tighter and with his other hand he reached for her hand that was closest to him and intertwined their fingers. He brought it to his lips and placed slow, delicate kisses on it."

"Baby, you are safe. I promise. You have nothing to fear when you are with me. You are most definitely wanted."

Candice leaned her head on his shoulder and couldn't help the tingle of happiness creeping up her spine. She felt her nipples tighten into hard little knobs. He continued, "But I don't understand why that would make you cry."

She gently brought his hand down and pulled it so both of his arms were surrounding her.

"Just the few days we've been together have been the happiest I've had since Alex and I were in college. I think I was crying because I feel so stupid at times for allowing myself to be mistreated." Landon held her tighter. "For allowing myself to be mistreated, violated, beaten and misused."

Landon was motionless and silent. What could he say to that?

Candice fought for the words so she could finally release the demons.

"You are not stupid, Candice." He said and even more gently he asked, "Why did you stay after the first time?"

"You have to understand Landon; I grew up in a very loving home. I never saw my father mistreat or disrespect my mother in any way. But what I did see was two people who honored their vows…I was brought up to believe that the man was the head of the house and the wife obeyed her husband." She took a deep breath and continued. "In my own way I felt I was honoring my vows and my parents by staying, however warped and twisted my marriage was. I thought if I left that it would be my fault for not doing my part in making it work."

"How did you end up marrying him?"

"I was young and naïve. He was charming and my parents loved him. He painted a wonderful picture of how great we would be together. 'We will be a powerful couple' he would say. We got married, he thought it was best that I leave school and become a proper wife. I know it sounds crazy, but I so much wanted to be a good wife to him. Before I realized it, I was estranged from all my friends and family except my parents. I guess he needed me to have their

189

example constantly in front of me." Candice turned more towards Landon. "The first time…" Her voice broke.

Landon's heart beat wildly. He was almost afraid for her to continue. His stomach was in knots. Never in his life had he wanted to kill someone, but he wanted to kill Devin Freedman for ever being in the same air space as Candice.

Candice composed herself and with a new found strength she continued. "The first time he hit me I realized I had no one to turn to. All my friends, Alex, and my close family members were no longer in my life."

"Why didn't you go to your parents?"

"I couldn't. I didn't want to burden them with the guilt that they had approved our match without reservations. So I tried my best to be a 'good wife.' I did what he asked, I dressed like he wanted me to, I was the perfect host, but still it was never good enough. Anything that went wrong with his work, he blamed on me. I was hospitalized twice and everyone knew me in the ER. It's amazing how it is so easy for people to ignore what is staring them in the face or pretend they don't see the obvious."

"I'm so sorry Candice. You didn't deserve any of that."

"It's taken a very long time and some therapy but I realize that now. I was letting his insecurities affect me and my self esteem."

"Was he always so awful?"

Yes, but I was able to tolerate it better after I had an outlet. He allowed me to paint freely after his boss saw one of my paintings hanging in our house. The owner of the art gallery is a good friend of Devin's boss and they both are art collectors. Devin agreed to it because he was up for a promotion. The night I saw Alex was the first night showcasing my collection." Candice wiped away a tear and instinctively Landon held her tighter and kissed her forehead. She smiled weakly and continued.

"I'm convinced Alex saved my life that night. If she had not have been there I'm sure he would have been especially violent. He hated anything good that happened to me. Success did not come easily to him and to watch me all evening as the center of attention, was driving him absolutely mad. I only hate that he assaulted Alex."

Landon knew the story from there. It was only a few days after that night that he'd met Candice. It's a wonder that she was able to function at all after leaving an abusive animal like Devin. She must have been scared to death. He was so glad Joshua had beaten the shit out of Devin that night. The guy deserved so much more.

"When I met you Landon, I was so surprised at how comfortable I was with you. You gave me hope that I could be whole again." She wiped her face again and smiled. "Now I'm here in your arms about to go off to Europe and live some of the dreams I'd given up." She sat up a bit so she could look at him.

"I'm really glad you tricked me into going on the trip and I'm especially glad that you are coming with me. But do you think I can get some clothes soon?"

His heart was filled with Candice. Her smile was a delicious invitation to kiss her. So he did. Slow at first, nibbling her lips and kissing the corners of her smile. He kissed the places where the tears fell. "No more tears Baby. I got you."

Candice sought out Landon's lips. She'd never shared her story with anyone. She wanted Landon to know that though she was once broken, she was healing and she was no longer afraid. He helped her know that she was worthy and she was in love with him and didn't want her past to spook him.

Candice knew that he had a life in London and hers was in Baton Rouge, but while she was with him she was ready to enjoy being free to make her own decisions. And right now she wanted to kiss and be kissed senselessly.

Chapter 20

Lucky Fourteen

"Thanks for meeting with me on such short notice Landon but I wanted to go over things before we meet with Global Green Industries. They acquired the structures in a takeover. The CEO was only interested in selling to a company who would restore and renew the area. As a matter of fact, he insisted it be in the contract." Ethan was eager to get the deal closed and begin restoring some of the buildings that have been an eyesore over the past decade.

"No problem Ethan, I had an errand to run a couple of blocks away so this was perfect timing." He told Candice he would be right back, but more than an hour passed and they were still at it. He called her to tell her he would be later than expected.

"I hope you are as excited about this opportunity as I am. I know it's a lot of money, but the projections indicate we will soon recover the initial capital as the area is renewed. You have a list of my credentials plus I'm sure you've run a background check on me and my company." Ethan gave a wry smile to Landon."

"Yes, I did." Landon hesitated before offering a smile in return.

It wasn't so unusual for acquaintances to go into business together, but Landon had known Ethan for only about 6 months. They'd met at an air safety conference in New York. Ethan owned a small private airport located in Brisbane. He was one of the presenters at the conference. The two were introduced by a mutual friend and found they both were born in Massachusetts and worked in the UK, though Ethan had grown up with his mother in Albany, NY. Both men were ready to leave the UK and their current line of work and began researching new business opportunities. When the opportunity presented itself to buy the company that owned a dying portion of Boston, they both were interested—Ethan for the business opportunities and Landon for more sentimental reasons.

His uncle Cortland took him and Joshua to that neighborhood all the time. It was where his uncle went to get away from the "society stiffs" as he'd called them.

It was difficult to believe that his uncle and his dad were brothers. They were like night and day—their physical appearance as well as their personalities. His Uncle Cortland was dark and his dad was very light, but more than that, his uncle didn't want any part of the strict confinements he felt upper-class socialites represented. His dad, on the other hand, though he resented the lifestyle, either refused or didn't know how to reject it. Consequently his father was swallowed up by it while Cortland spent his time working with his hands and teaching his nephews how to really live.

Landon, however, knew that at one time his uncle and dad were as close as he and Joshua were now. He also knew that his mom was most likely the reason why the brothers drifted apart. Uncle Cortland hate being around his mother. Landon figured it was probably because she represented everything that made him hate "society folk," as he called them. He often told his mom that her constant need to be perfect only accentuated her vivid flaws.

Landon knew that was one of the reasons why he loved Genius, the area of downtown they would revitalize. It was called Genius because it was there before the gaudy, sleek and polished office buildings infiltrated the area.

He would hate to see the buildings torn down and replaced with vulgar architecture that housed so many offices these days. There was no integrity in design anymore, just flashy buildings to appeal to the vanity gods.

Landon picked up a few design ideas and asked Ethan a few questions about them.

Candice couldn't stand it anymore. She needed her clothes. Her stuff! She prided herself on her style and ability to always look classically chic. She loved to shop, but in order for her to do more of it she needed clothes to wear. Landon was still in his meeting. He'd told her a good friend of his was the hotel manager at the Waldorf nearby and that's where the luggage was delivered. Who says she couldn't get it herself.

She could take a cab over, have lunch and return before Landon was done. If he showed up, they could have lunch together.

Donned in the travel clothes she'd worn to London, Candice scribbled Landon a note saying she was going to get her bags and would be back after she grabbed lunch.

The moment she was greeted at the door of the Waldorf, she was ensconced in luxury. She wondered if she should eat lunch there or try to find a place a bit more reasonable, then decided she would live it up and enjoy a meal there.

There was no sense in getting her bags and dragging them to the table therefore she resigned to get them after her meal. It was still fairly early for lunch so she was surprised to see the place so crowded. They seated her at the bar until a table became available. The gentleman tending bar had such a thick Scottish accent that she had difficulty understanding him. From what she could gather there was some sort of convention of sorts in town which explained why the restaurant was so crowded.

"Hello, Sweetheart." There was no British accent in the greeting that she knew so well. Fear gripped her so acutely that she couldn't form a word. She looked up at the bartender but he walked away to give them privacy. She felt a vise-like grip on her elbow the moment she tried to turn to move. "There is no place to go, Baby."

"What are you doing here, Devin?" Her tone was low and controlled. She looked around and no one seemed to notice the grip Devin had on her arm. He'd perfected the art of being able to hurt her without drawing attention to himself.

"I came for you, Candice. Do you think I believed that story you and Phoenix came up with?"

198

Tsk Tsk Tsk… "You should know me better than that." She tried to pull away from him again. He eased onto the barstool next to her and with his other hand, placed a silver pistol discreetly in his lap.

"Now don't go making me ruin all these nice folks day by having them witness a husband kill his wife in a jealous rage." He looked around the room and then back at her. "Now…you're going to get off the stool and join me upstairs where I can show you how much I've been missing you."

"You're going to have to kill me right here before I go anywhere with you."

Devin raised his eyebrows and smiled mockingly.

"Got a little spunk in ya now. I like that. It gives me a hard on to beat the fight out of you."

She jerked her arm away from him, but before she could turn to leave, a group of kids came into the restaurant with several adults. One of the kids walked up to her.

"Hi. I lost a tooth. Seeee!" The little girl opened her mouth and smiled really big so Candice could see the missing tooth at the bottom.

Devin leaned in much too close to her and whispered in an icy tone, "Look at that innocent face. You sure you want to get shot right before her eyes."

Candice pulled her head away from Devin and focused on the little girl. "Yes I do see." The child's mom walked over, smiled politely and retrieved the little girl who was about four years old. "She sees it Emily. Come on, Auntie Virginia wants to see it too." She mouthed to Candice, "Sorry."

Candice didn't try to move away again. Devin was very capable of shooting her in front of a room full of people.

"Now slowly get off the stool and stay at my side." He grabbed her harshly by the elbow again with the other hand in his coat pocket. She assumed that's where he put the gun.

Where was he taking her? How did he know where to find her and what was he going to do to her?

He turned her towards the elevators and she looked wildly about for Landon. Maybe he was done with his meeting and had come for her luggage. She looked towards the concierges' desk. There was no Landon. She looked towards the door. Not a familiar face in sight.

"Your lover boy can't save you now." He growled and tugged her hard to keep up with him as they walked towards the elevator.

The ding announcing the arrival of the elevator made her heart beat fast and the blood drain from her face. She felt light headed. The lack of sleep combined with the sudden arrival of Devin was causing her to feel faint. She refused to faint. She refused to appear weak in front of him.

The elevator doors opened and a crowd of people got off. She looked around her and noticed other people waiting to get on as well. Candice stepped into the elevator car with Devin and the other travelers. She felt the pocket of her coat vibrate. She looked around the car at the faces and as she eased her hand in her pocket, she wondered if these were the last faces besides Devin's that she would see.

"Visitin' ar' ya?" The man standing next to Devin asked. Devin didn't respond. The man tapped Devin on the shoulder, giving Candice time to push the "talk" button on her phone and remove her hand from her pocket. Maybe, just maybe it was Landon and she hoped to God that he would wonder why she wasn't answering. "Visitin' ar ya?" The man asked again after getting Devin's attention.

"Yes, my wife and I just arrived today."

The elevator dinged and stopped for the first time on the third floor, then the seventh, ninth, and by the time it stopped on the fourteenth floor, there was only an elderly woman carrying several shopping bags.

Candice hesitated a moment before Devin darted his eyes to the old woman then back at Candice.

"Lucky fourteen, huh, Devin?"

Devin narrowed his eyes at Candice and squeezed her arm tighter as he pulled her down the corridor.

"You're in 1035 and I'm in 1036…Sir?"

"I'm sorry, what did you say?"

"I said you're in 1035 and I'm in 1036." She held the card in front of him but he was too preoccupied to notice. "Dixon, what is it?"

He was still facing the elevator when she spoke again. "Did you see someone you know?"

"I don't know…It couldn't have been…" His voice trailed off before he tuned to Gloria to retrieve the key. Dixon Phoenix looked at his secretary and said, "I could have sworn I just saw my daughter-in-law's best friend get on the elevator with a gentleman."

"Maybe it was her. Does she travel here often?" Gloria asked as she too, looked towards the elevators.

"I'm not sure. All I know of her is that she is an artist in Baton Rouge. The jetlag must be getting to me. Come on, let's get some rest and meet later for dinner." Dixon wanted to meet with his son and decided to give him a call after he got some rest. The long flights tired him out more now since he'd gotten older.

Landon hadn't realized so much time had passed. He looked at his watch and wondered what Candice was doing. He missed her already and couldn't wait to get back to her. *Did she miss him?*

When they talked earlier, he had every intention of telling her that he loved her. But, instead, when he sought her out he found her crying. Candice opened up to him and exposed some pretty raw wounds. He felt that if he would have told her that he was in love with her after their talk, she would think he was only saying it because he felt sorry for her.

He looked at his watch again. *He needed to wrap this up.*

Ethan wanted to go over every detail of the contract they'd prepared for Global Green. Though the two of them would have a 50/50 share of the business profits, Ethan would be the face of Enrich Corp, the business they created for the real estate project. Landon heard Ethan say something but his mind was not on the contracts or the project. He needed to call and check on Candice. She may think he was blowing her off and left her in the house alone in a country she was not familiar with. What the hell was he thinking?

"I'm sorry man, I've got to go." Landon stood from the conference table.

Ethan looked up at him.

"Everything ok?"

"There's just something I need to check on at home. Is there anything else I need to be here for before the meeting tomorrow with Global Green?"

"No I think we've covered everything. There is a couple of things I need to fax to you. Just sign them and send them back. Of course after we close the deal tomorrow we will have to set up shop in Boston, but most of that is in the works and the rest can be handled when you return from vacation."

"Ok, Ethan. I guess I'll see you in the morning." They shook hands, Landon grabbed his briefcase, pulled out his phone and called Candice. The phone rang a couple of times and he thought maybe she wasn't near it. He was about to hang up with she answered. "Hey, I'm sorry it took so long but I'm—"

The sounds were muffled as if she had butt dialed him, but he was the one who had called her. "Candice?" Why did he hear people in the background? Where was she? The sounds faded in and out. He was about to hang up when he heard her say something. "Candice...Candice?" The line went dead.

Chapter 21

Something to Worry About

Landon was torn between going back to his flat to check on Candice and going to the hotel to pick up her luggage. Something wasn't right. He could feel it. Traffic was horrible and he cursed himself again for leaving her alone. He could have had someone from the hotel send the bags over.

That phone call kept playing in his head. Why would he have heard people in the background? It sounded like she said the number 14, but why hadn't she said anything?

His cell phone rang and he put it to his ear before checking who it was. "Candice?"

"Why would Candice be calling you? You aren't with her?" It was Joshua.

Disappointed and frustrated, it took Landon a moment to process the questions Joshua asked.

"I had a business meeting. I'm headed home now."

"Is everything ok? You sound worried."

"It's nothing. What's up? Didn't I just talk to you this morning?" Landon was driving at turtle speed and his frustration level was on warp.

Landon was about to come up with an excuse to get off the phone when Joshua spoke. "I talked to Mom."

He'd remembered Joshua telling him about that guy thinking their dad was sick. "What'd she say?"

"She didn't say much and avoided the question when I asked her about dad not going to any of their functions lately."

"Figures." Landon scoffed. "Was dad there?"

"No, actually I was surprised when she said Dad had a business meeting in London. Has he tried to contact you?"

"No, I told you I haven't talked to either of them in a while."

"Maybe he will call you when he gets settled. I wonder what kind of business meeting he has out there."

Landon began to wonder himself. It could be very possible that the CEO that he and Ethan were meeting with was his father.

"Hello? Landon, you there?"

"Yea, man, I'm here. I was just thinking about something. I am supposed to meet with the CEO of

Global Green Industries tomorrow, but all the paperwork lists the CEO as Brian Logan." Traffic was moving a little better but it was starting to drizzle. He was ready to leave the cold rainy climate for something a little milder.

"What kind of meeting does an airline pilot have with Global Green?"

"The kind that will help an airline pilot give up his wings."

"What the hell man! When did you decide all of this? When were you going to tell me? Dude!"

"Damn Joshua, calm down. You sound like I just told you I've decided to sell crack." He took a deep breath and continued. "I've been thinking about it for a while and an opportunity came up to partner with a guy I met."

"What guy?" Joshua was sounding as if Landon was his kid or something.

He spoke in a patronizing voice, "His name is Ethan Powers. He's from Massachusetts, but grew up in Albany."

"That's his credentials?"

"Will you give me more credit than that Joshua? I had the guy checked out. He's quite a wiz in the business world. His main business is an airport he started from scratch in Brisbane, but he dabbles in other things as well. Ethan's background is in architecture, highly sought after, but he felt like he was selling out by designing skyscrapers with no character."

"So what is it that the two of you are meeting with Global Green for?"

"Global Green is the owner of a company that has possession of a dilapidated area of Boston. We're going to buy the company and therefore own a very profitable piece of real estate after we revive it…So do you know if Dad is involved with Global Green?"

"I'm not sure. I'm like you Landon. I didn't want anything to do with the family business. Why do you think we live on a yacht and own sports bars?" There was a pause in the conversation again. "So did you tell her?"

"I'm going to tell her Joshua."

"Chicken shit." Joshua didn't say it to provoke Landon but to tease him a bit because he understood how scared he was to tell Candice he was in love with her. He'd gone through the same thing with Alex.

"Actually I was all set to tell her, then we talked and she laid some heavy stuff on me. It just wasn't the right time."

"It's always the right time Landon."

There was finally a break in traffic that allowed him to actually go the speed limit. He was almost home.

"I'm going to make it right Josh. Now go tend to my beautiful sister-in-law and stop bothering me." Landon was about to click off the phone when Joshua asked him a question. "Where will you two be for Candice's birthday next week?"

Landon had completely forgotten the trip to Europe was supposed to be a birthday gift for Candice. He hadn't even bothered to ask her when it was. He felt like an ass. "I'm not sure where we will be. Getting out of London seems to be a task in itself with lost luggage and delayed meetings."

"Alex mentioned she wanted to meet up with the two of you so we all can celebrate her birthday together."

Landon rolled his eyes. "And what if I wanted to spend Candice's birthday alone with just she and I?"

"Yea, that wouldn't matter to Alexandra and you know it."

"Just as I thought. When exactly is her birthday anyway?"

"It's a week from tomorrow. We can hang out over the weekend and the following week. So that gives you a week and a day to get your shit together before we get wherever you will be."

"It doesn't seem like we have much choice in the matter so I'm not sure why you even bothered to ask."

"I didn't ask if we could come, I asked where you would be."

"Well I will think about telling you. In the meantime, stop calling every five minutes. I'm never going to get to talk to Candice if I'm always talking to you! Now good bye!" Landon clicked off the phone and turned into his garage.

Like a movie when the sound is muffled and the action is taking place in slow motion, Landon felt detached from reality. She'd left a note and he immediately knew Candice was in trouble.

Hey Landon if you
come home first, I'm
at the hotel picking up my
luggage and having lunch.
Call me! I'll be waiting!

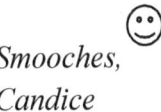

Smooches,
Candice

"Candice!...Candice!" He knew there would be no answer or anyone to be found as he took the stairs two at a time. She was not there. *My God where is she. The phone call...*

Landon snatched his keys off of the counter, pulled out his phone and dialed Candice again. It went straight to voice mail. "Hey Candice, it's me. Call me back please. I'm a little worried about you."

That was a lie. He was a lot worried. More than that, he had a gut feeling that something was terribly wrong.

As he pulled out of the garage, he tried to take some deep breaths and stay focused. She had left a note so he knew where she'd gone. It could be just her service provider that prevented her from getting good reception. *Yes. Yes. Calm down Phoenix, you're overreacting.* Landon was glad the traffic wasn't bad and the hotel was near his flat. He tried Candice again and got the voicemail. He looked in his contacts and found the number he was looking for.

"Colin...Yea, it's Landon....Ok...Hey, did my friend Candice come down to pick up her luggage?... Ok..." Colin put Landon on hold. "Yea, I'm here...she didn't?...I'll be there in a moment."

Colin was the closest friend Landon had in London. The first time Landon flew from London to New York, Colin was on his way to meet a woman who'd stayed at his hotel four months prior. The two communicated via email and phone since her visit to London.

Colin was so nervous to finally see her after such a long time that he had a mild heart attack on the flight to the states. Landon was just coming out of the lavatory when he saw Colin collapse into the aisle. He performed CPR and got him stable until they landed. The ambulance was waiting when they arrived in New York and told Colin he would have died if Landon hadn't intervened.

Colin insisted he repay Landon in some way. Landon refused at first but when Colin offered him to use any of the facilities at the Waldorf he relented. So when he had days off at home in London, he worked out and used the pool at the hotel. Colin also let him have things delivered there when Landon didn't want things to go to his home address.

During the last few blocks of the ride, Landon thought again about the phone call. He'd heard her say something. *Damit what was it!*

213

Just as efficient as ever, the valets were waiting eagerly to assist. He jumped out of the car and tossed the valet the keys. "The name's Phoenix."

The doorman opened the door and greeted Landon warmly. The older man had been a fixture there for decades, everyone loved him. Landon grew quite fond of him as well and always made it a point to stop and chat with him for a moment. Today, however, Landon spoke to him quickly and walked toward the concierges' desk. He saw his friend Colin walking towards him.

"What's going on my friend? You seemed troubled on the phone?" Colin took Landon's hand and shook it firmly.

"I'm not sure Colin. A friend of mine said she was coming here for lunch and to pick up the luggage I had delivered from the airline."

Colin asked the man at the desk if she'd picked up the luggage. She had not.

Landon described her to them and what he thought she may be wearing. Neither had seen her.

"Is there something wrong Landon? It's not like you to be this worked up." Colin asked.

"I just have a feeling that something is wrong." He looked around and noticed all the people. "Why is it so crowded?"

"There are several groups having meetings here this week…Let's check the restaurant over here." They walked over to the restaurant closest to the lobby. The hostess stand was crowded so they went to the bar first.

"Patrick." Colin called out to the bartender and he walked over with a broad smile. He was asked if he'd seen a woman fitting the description Landon gave again.

Landon felt as if he was filling out a missing person's report. He didn't like the feeling one bit.

"Ay, no. I'd say I would have remembered a lovely pixie like that aye."

The two men started to walk towards the hostess stand when Patrick said, "Maybe Robbie saw her; he was here before me. I just got started."

Robbie walked over and they started the process again of describing Candice.

"Lovely thing isn't she." His accent was thick but Landon knew what he said.

He'd seen her!

"Is she still here?" Landon asked as he walked to the dining area not waiting for a reply.

"No." Robbie called out after him as he pulled out a towel and wiped off the bar top. "She left with a gentleman."

Landon stopped and moved towards the bar again. A knot formed in his stomach as he tried without much success to stay calm. He began rattling off questions at Robbie faster than the man could reply. Colin stepped in to calm the situation and ask Robbie to describe the man while Landon looked at them, feeling useless.

"Oh my God." Landon whispered in disbelief as Robbie described the man.

"Do you know who she was with?" Colin asked concerned because of Landon's reaction to the news. He walked around to the other side of the bar before he got an answer. Colin reached the cash register and pulled out charge card receipts.

Landon looked at Colin but all he could see was Candice's face after he'd kissed her goodbye and told her he would be back shortly.

"It could only be her ex-husband Devin Freedman." He said, finally answering Colin's question.

Just as Landon said the name, Colin held up a receipt with the same name.

Chapter 22

Remembering

Something was tied tightly over her eyes. A blindfold. It was a familiar tactic he used to illicit as much fear as he could. Devin figured she would be more afraid if she didn't know what harm he would inflict on her. Candice knew she was in the hotel room. She could feel the richness of a chair. She'd seen the rich plush texture of it before he struck her--for old time's sakes she assumed. She'd known it would come.

He'd followed her all the way to London because he believed she belonged to him. Her head hurt and she could feel something on her chin—blood most likely. She tried to touch her mouth to wipe it away and because it throbbed, but found her hands were tied.

How had she remained with this monster for so long? The moment he shoved her into the hotel room and slapped her hard across the face, eight years of hell came flooding back to her mind.

Though she didn't think he'd hit her more than the one time, it was as if she could feel the bruises on her back and legs again. She remembered how she had to carefully avoid people when they greeted her too warmly. She remembered every slap, kick and punch. She remembered vividly how she had to carefully control herself from flinching due to sudden movements of strangers. She remembered every hateful word. Every time her heart raced when she heard the key in the door and wondered what kind of mood he would be in and what kind of condition she would be in by the time she went to bed—she remembered.

Candice remembered the aching stomach from vomiting so intensely after the beatings. Remembering made her eyes feel puffy and bloodshot. Instinctively she stuck her tongue out to feel her bottom lip, sure to taste the remnants of blood from the busted lip that he'd inflicted. She wasn't sure how much time had passed since he forced her upstairs because she didn't recall being blindfolded or tied to a chair.

Just being in the same space with him, allowed her to remember the fear, the sleepless nights, the loneliness and the tears that refused to come. Refused to give him the satisfaction of knowing she was hurting inside.

Devin was a coward and she knew it. He perfected the art of charm for fear of confrontation. He worked hard at kissing the right asses at work for fear of being unsuccessful. He had the perfect wife, home and car for fear of feeling inferior to others. He beat the hell out of his wife because he was afraid she could see right through him. She did and she hated *him* for it. Hated him for being so weak. His weakness disgusted her, but in order for her to survive and move beyond the clutches of Devin, she had to let the hatred go.

Even after just a few months of counseling and support groups, she no longer detested him. Though many would think she had ample cause to hate him, she was wracked with guilt from it. It had taken her a while to get over the guilt she felt for hating him so intently—now she was working on the negative feelings she had for herself for feeling guilty for that bastard. Vicious cycle.

Eight years of marriage with this man. No, he was no man. Her father was a man. Landon was a man. Devin sure as hell didn't deserve that title.

Candice remembered the hellish years with Devin but her mind was over powered by the past few days with Landon.

Landon.

Where was he?

He'd promised that she would be safe with him. Tucked in the safety of him, he'd told her she no longer needed to be afraid. Although her life was being

219

threatened and she was tied to a chair, she believed Landon. They had a connection; she felt it was more than just a sexual bond or chemistry. Candice had been able to be freer with Landon than she was with herself.

How was that possible?

She didn't know the answer to that question, but what she did know, was that she was in love with Landon Phoenix and no matter how he felt about her she was sure he would come for her.

Just the thought of him and the possibility that he was at that very moment looking for her, made her no longer afraid. He gave her peace. Even now, in the midst of Devin's madness, she was at peace because she hadn't passed up the opportunity to share something special with Landon. Something she'd never experienced. Something she so desperately needed to help her erase the residual film Devin still left clinging to her.

She could sense him moving towards her, smell the heavy cologne he wore that tended to linger unwanted in her nostrils. Candice imagined him leering at her, eager to make her suffer for whatever he felt she should be punished for. Devin snatched off the blindfold, pulling a hair or two with it. As she tried to focus her eyes on her surroundings she saw him walk away from her. Apparently he wanted her to see what he was doing.

He was like a kid acting up in school. What good was it to act a fool when there was no one to witness it? It was just the two of them in the room from what she could see and he'd either just arrived or he was preparing to leave. Candice hoped it was the former and not the latter.

The phone, her coat and the contents of her purse were spread across the bed. The mess of it all was oddly out of place on such a stately made bed. He was obviously searching for something, her passport perhaps. He'd told her he was taking her home.

Home.

That was it—the comfort she felt with Landon. Candice felt at home with him. The feeling was so foreign to her that she hadn't recognized it before now. Though her face burned where he'd hit her and her head felt as if it weighted down with rocks, she couldn't stop the smile that interrupted her lips, though she was still angry from being taken against her will. Thinking of Landon comforted her and that made her smile even in the midst of madness.

Devin dug into a small pocket on the inside of her purse and snatched out the passport. His face contorted into a sickening image of a hyena. He turned to face her and just as quickly as the deranged smile appeared; it disappeared when he turned towards her.

It was as if the smile on her face in the middle of him attempting to hurt her actually pained him. It was brief but she saw it, saw the fleeting look of fear that ran across *his* eyes. He was afraid.

Candice's chest heaved and fell as if someone was pumping courage like air, into her lungs with a bellow. Her eyes didn't leave his and the sweet smile from thoughts of feeling at home with Landon, increased into a toothy grin not unlike that of a lunatic let loose. Maybe she was. Maybe she'd not really recovered and had finally snapped. Maybe this was her time to go crazy on *him* like Tina did with Ike. Maybe this was her time to be in control of the situation.

Her hands were still tied behind her back but the intensity in her eyes held him rooted to his spot. She refused to look away—refused to give him the satisfaction of being intimidated by him. Her sockets burned and her lids ached to release the stare. Tears spilled over the rim and blazed slow trails of heat down her face. The crazed smile remained.

Devin blinked and with false bravado, he pretended her tears were from the Candice that shook when he passed too near to her. He walked towards her and hesitantly leaned over the chair where she sat. Her

222

eyes never wavered. With the pad of his thumb he roughly wiped away tear. He leaned in closer and whispered into her ear, his breath hot, stale and laced with alcohol. "Don't be afraid, Baby, we will be home soon."

He stood up in front of her again and looked down. She began to laugh. She didn't know why but she laughed loud and heartily.

Devin's face was instantly a glowering mask of rage. He slapped her hard across her face. She knew it was coming. It was his way. She knew the signs. His fist would open and close as if it ached to slam into the side of her face. But she knew better. She knew that he felt a slap across the face was one of the most humiliating punishments, aside from... She refused to even think about it. Instead she looked up at him with soft eyes and gave him a pitiful smirk.

Devin placed his hands on the arms of the chair and braced himself there, inches away from her face. She smiled. "Hit me again. You know you want to." She gave a short contemptible sigh and turned her face away from his as if she was telling him to get on with it.

Devin grabbed her face, squeezing hard, and turned it back towards him. "Don't you turn away from me, you bitch, as if you feel sorry for me. You must

223

have forgotten who you are dealing with. I'm not that pale-faced Ken doll you are screwing!"

Fury nearly paralyzed Candice. Her lips shook as she tried to smile even though he was squeezing so tightly near her mouth. Evidently he took her shaking lips as a sign of panic so he let her go as if he'd proven his point. He stood again and turned and walked towards the bathroom.

"I am not afraid of you, Devin." Her voice was strong and sure. He stopped and turned towards her again. He lifted an eyebrow as if he didn't believe her. For the first time she really got a good look at him. He wore the same blue suit from the Baton Rouge encounter. It was a bit disheveled, the tie had a stain on it and there was a button missing on his shirt. She looked at his shoes. They were brown and scuffed. Devin prided himself on his appearance so his clothes didn't make sense to her. He had the look of a desperate man down on his luck.

He interrupted her appraisal of him when he spoke. "Well your trembling begs to differ, Sweetheart."

The term of endearment disgusted her. Her eyes traveled the length of him from foot to head and she shook her head with that same look of pity she had before.

"I feel sorry for you, Devin. You are a weak, cowardly bastard and when Landon finds me here and sees what you've done to me," She said the last part slow and clearly, "it will be *you* who will tremble…right before he whips your ass."

Chapter 23

Dad?

Still standing near the restaurant, Landon looked at his phone again. The last call he'd made to Candice, when she picked up, was nearly an hour ago.

"Should I call Scotland Yard?" Colin asked his friend, very concerned. He'd never seen Landon lose control. Of course he'd seen him upset, but never to the point where he was irrational. Poor Robbie, Colin had to give him the rest of the day off because Landon grabbed the man and shook the daylights out of him demanding answers about where that Devin fella' had taken Candice.

"And tell them what? That my girlfriend won't answer her phone? I have nothing other than she was sitting here with a guy, then she wasn't."

The fact that Landon called Candice his girlfriend did not escaped Colin. He'd known just from Landon's behavior that the woman must be very important to him. Now things were even more muddled in Colin's head. But before he had a chance to think about it further they were interrupted.

"Landon?"

Both men turned towards the voice. Landon's frustrated frown turned to one of surprise to see his father walking towards him. *Could this day get any stranger?* "Dad?"

The older Phoenix approached his son with a cautious smile, unsure how welcomed his presence would be. Their relationship had improved only slightly over the past year and Dixon wasn't sure if it was because Landon no longer cared enough to bother being upset or if he was trying to give him another chance to be a dad to him again. Dixon took a gamble it was the latter and opted not to extend his hand for the usual formal greeting that was the norm for them, but instead he opened his arms, not ashamed to admit to himself or anyone that he missed hugging his son.

Colin knew Landon didn't see his parents often and for the longest time he thought they were deceased because Landon very rarely spoke of them; and when he had, it was in reference to a distant memory. It was only recently that he found out they were still living. Right after Landon's brother, Joshua, got married; Landon mentioned his mom had greatly disapproved of the match. It was then, Colin realized Landon's parents still were alive and well in Boston.

He watched the two men. The older approached cautiously as if he were bracing himself for rejection.

"You hugged your old man like you're glad to see him, son!" The older man said.

"I am, but more than that, I'm surprised as hell. What are you doing here, Dad? Are you here on business? Someone said you've been sick." Landon had so many questions, but he knew he couldn't stop now to go into detail about anything but Candice.

"Well I'm a little surprised myself. I thought I was seeing things again. What are you doing at the Waldorf, Son?" Dixon was as surprised as Landon and had as many questions. He was just coming downstairs to walk around a bit because he was restless. He'd planned on calling Landon a little later to see if he would join him for a drink before dinner.

Landon remembered his friend standing there and turned to introduce him to his father. "Colin this is my fa—" Before he finished the introduction, Landon turned back to Dixon puzzled, "What do you mean, 'seeing things again'?" He thought about the conversation he and Joshua had earlier and wondered if his dad really was ill.

Dixon smiled, scratched his temple and turned towards the elevator. "Well when Gloria and I were checking in…"

"Gloria?" Landon interrupted to ask.

Dixon turned back to Landon and tried to sound as casual as he could and wondered why he felt a need to do so; men traveled with their secretaries all the time. "Yes, that's my secretary. I told you I'm here on business." Landon didn't seem to require any further explanation so he looked back towards the elevator as if looking that way would rewind the clock and have the woman appear there again. He continued, "I could have sworn I saw Alex's friend get on that elevator with a gentleman."

"Candice? You saw her get on the elevator? Oh my God...No! That bastard has her in a hotel room!"

With no regard to where he was going, Landon rushed towards the elevators. Dixon looked towards Colin with a deep frown on his face, searching for some sort of explanation for his son's behavior, but Colin's long stride was only two steps behind Landon. Dixon followed the two men with his eyes, too stunned to move. He heard the ding of from the elevator just as Colin caught up with Landon.

What in the world was going on, Dixon thought. Then he remembered he'd mentioned Candice's name right before Landon took off towards the elevators. Was the lady he saw actually Candice? Why was she here and why in the world would Landon be chasing after her if the woman was with another man?

He also remembered what he knew about Candice and immediately sensed she was in some sort of danger. *But what was she doing in London?* The question kept coming back to him. The way his son reacted to the news, he could guess what she was doing in London. Landon was taken with Candice from the time he'd met her, so if Candice was supposed to be here with Landon then there was definitely trouble.

Dixon walked up to the two men arguing.

"Landon I can't let you go tearing through my hotel!" Colin tried not to yell, but it was nearly impossible.

"If I have to knock down every damn door to find her then that's what I will do." Landon moved towards the open elevator door, but was restrained when Colin grabbed his arm.

"The bloody hell you will, Phoenix! Calm down and listen to reason." Colin looked towards the older man, seeking some assistance to prevent Landon from acting rashly.

Dixon stood in front of Landon. "Listen to reason Son; knocking on doors gives the person behind it an advantage."

Landon pulled his arm free from Colin's grip and looked into eyes that were not so unlike his own, except there was no hint of blue in Dixon's. He relented a little, still a bit surprised his father was there at all. He would make a brief attempt to "listen to reason," but he tried to make his father understand what was going on first.

"Dad her ex-husband has her!" Landon didn't yell but his voice was urgent—expectant. He expected that was enough to be said. Though saying it out loud again caused fear to slice through his abdomen.

"Ok son, but you have to be smart about this thing."

"Ok? It's not ok, Dad—you have no idea what he is capable of."

Dixon placed his hand caringly yet firmly on Landon's shoulder, partly to show support and also to keep him from running off.

"I know Landon, and we will find her, but your friend here is right. You can't go tearing through the hotel like a maniac. Like I said, that will give him an advantage you can't afford to give him."

"Dad we don't have time for this!"

"Stop and think Landon! Even if you happen to find the room she's in—"

Landon interrupted his father and looked from Dixon to Colin. "I heard her say, 'fourteen' when I called her. Maybe she was giving me a clue as to what floor she was on."

"Good… good. We know where to look first, but like I was saying, if you start beating down doors he has an advantage over you."

Landon heard the ding of one of the elevators arriving again and turned toward it, ignoring his father and the grip he had on his shoulder. Dixon held London in place. Landon looked at his father's hand on his should then at his father. He was stunned by his father's strength.

"Landon Phoenix! You will stop and listen to me damit!"

Landon stared at his father momentarily taken aback. People milling about turned to look in their direction, but the disturbance wasn't dramatic enough to cause more than a cursory glance.

Landon never heard his father yell. Never. Not at him or Joshua and definitely not his mother. He didn't know quite how to feel about it, but Dixon didn't let up to give him an instant to try to sort it out. "What do you think he will do when you show up? Just send Candice out gift wrapped for you?"

Landon just stared at Dixon, but Dixon could feel Landon's shoulders relax though he didn't loosen his hold. He continued, "That man beat the hell out of his wife. I assume he traveled all this way for a reason. Until you know what that reason is, I suggest we do this another way."

"Dad, what if he hurts her?" Landon's voice lost its edge momentarily.

"We're not going to let that happen, son." He squeezed Landon's shoulder reassuring him before he moved his hand back to his own side, believing Landon was at least willing to be reasonable.

Dixon turned to Colin, whom had been standing aside watching the two men. "Did you say this was *your* hotel?"

"Yes Sir, I'm Colin Moore. I'm the general manager of this hotel."

With no time for pleasantries, Dixon was immediately all business. "Do you have cameras on each floor?" Landon and Colin looked at each other, both wondering why they hadn't thought of that.

"Yes, Sir!" Colin instantaneously led the group of men across the lobby and down a corridor to the security offices.

"Landon what time was it when you spoke to Candice last?"

"I didn't speak to her, but it was about 11:07."

Colin, have them check the fourteenth floor video around that time."

Landon had never seen his dad take charge. He'd never seen him conduct business either and wondered if he commanded attention and respect in the business world like he was doing at the moment. He was in awe of his father.

They watched the screen show the video of the hallway at three times the normal speed, in silence. Though Landon was sure everyone could hear his heart slamming against his chest.

Dixon, still acting as spokesman, tapped the security officer on the shoulder as he stood behind him viewing the screen. "Stop it here, please." Dixon's voice was slow and controlled. The screen stopped and played back at regular speed. "Rewind it a hair." Dixon commanded.

And there she was. Landon couldn't see her face but he would know her anywhere. She was wearing the outfit she'd traveled in—a cream-colored skirt that stopped above her ankle and a brown cable-knit sweater.

"That's her!" Landon all but shouted.

"Ok son, we got them. Let's see where they are going."

Landon gripped the chair he was leaning on when he saw Devin's hold on Candice's elbow. They stopped in front of a door and he watched Devin take out the key card from his pocket, look up and down the corridor and slide the card into the slot in the door.

What the hell was he waiting on? There she was. His woman. He'd promised to keep her safe and he failed. What would she think of him now? How would he be able to prove to her that as long as she allowed him to love her, she would be ok? Could he?

Landon watched the monitor as Devin opened the door and moved aside so Candice could walk in before him. She refused. At least now he knew for certain that she was there against her will. *Had he been worried about that?*

A roar shook the quiet monitoring room when Landon watched in helpless horror, Devin grab Candice roughly by the arm, shove her across the threshold and strike her hard across the face. Everyone was stunned by the carnal rage that escaped Landon as they all winced at the blow she received.

The hotel room door closed and the room number was visible—1409. Landon broke for the door and with the agility and speed of a much younger man; Dixon reached his son before he could leave the room.

235

"Dad, I did what you said. I found out where that bastard has Candice. Now get out of my way." His eyes blazed with rage and his jaw was steeled determination. "You saw what he did to her in an opened corridor. God knows what he has done to her behind closed doors!"

"Damnit Landon! Don't let your stubbornness get that woman hurt more than she has been already." He took a step closer to Landon, standing nearly eye to eye daring him to try to get by him.

"You're going to calm down and listen to me for once in your life!" Dixon relaxed his stance a bit, took a step back and turned to Colin. "You just saw a man force a woman into a hotel room against her will so don't give me any privacy laws bullshit."

Colin was just as upset as all the men watching and ached to get a hold of the man himself, though he knew that there would be none left of him if Landon reached him first. "What do you need?"

"Do you have a female on your security team?"

"Aye," Colin acknowledged.

As pissed and as anxious as he was, Landon was still in awe of his father's take control attitude.

"Get her dressed in a housekeeping outfit and make sure she has a master key."

Landon interrupted. "Why can't I just take the key and go in myself."

"What if he is near her and you bursting in the room causes him to do something rash like threaten her life?" Dixon knew that he had to do what he could to keep Landon from the man who had taken Candice. He knew Landon would probably try to kill the man.

"Her life is already in danger. She's with that animal."

"No son, we can't do it that way."

Landon wanted to punch the wall. He balled his hands into fists saving it for Devin Freedman instead.

Dixon continued, "If 'housekeeping' knocks on the door, it may cause him to move away from Candice, giving us a chance to get in there without her being harmed."

Colin was already on the phone arranging things. Everyone else kept their eyes on the monitor that showed a live feed of the door that separated Landon from the woman he loved.

Chapter 24

Until Death...

For some reason, the image of Charlie Chaplin beating the hell out of Devin with his cane, kept playing across Candice's mind. She imagined Charlie whacking Devin across the head, dropping him to his knees. Charlie would dance off in silent victory and just when Devin thought the coast was clear, Charlie would shuffle over to him and beat him down to the ground again. The cycle would continue until Devin just gave up and stayed down.

Candice knew that was Devin's problem, he wasn't smart enough to stay down when he thought someone had gotten the best of him. She knew for certain that's why he was in London. From the looks of him, he wasn't doing too well. She, on the other hand, was rid of him and the abuse, doing well and doing what she loved. She was happy and Devin knew it. He saw evidence of it when he saw her with Landon. Candice was sure that since then, envy had eaten him inside out. Now here he was, trying to physically inflict the pain on her that he was feeling for his own lowdown trifling life.

Candice's face still stung from his automatic and systematic assault she received as a result of the insult she antagonized him with. Her body was beginning to betray her; it wracked violently as fear snaked its way around her calm demeanor and was quickly turning it into a façade.

Devin's sanity seemed to be propped up only by a very loose and unreliable kickstand.

"Cowardly!...Weak?" He leaned over her. His face only inches from hers. His eyes were glassy and breath two-day-old-foul. "You threaten *me* with another man?" Devin stood up and reached for the buckle on his belt. Her eyes widened in surprise. A satanic smile unlike one she'd ever seen spread across his face.

"Oh, you don't feel the need to laugh anymore?" He taunted her.

He pulled the tucked end of the belt free from the buckle and took a step back. Candice pulled at the ties binding her wrists as panic began to block her breathing passages. Devin continued, "You threaten me with another man and you call me weak and a coward?" He removed the prong from the hole in the leather.

Were the ties loosening or was it her imagination?

239

"You whore! You adulteress! You are my wife! Your body belongs to me…to *me*!" Saliva sprayed from his mouth.

The leather was free from the buckle.

She didn't know if he planned to beat her with the belt or if…

Candice refused to even think about any other vile alternatives to a beating.

"I am not your wife Devin or have you forgotten?" Her hands were getting numb and she was afraid for the first time since he appeared at the bar, but she thought if she kept him talking it would distract him somehow. She was afraid of the deranged man who was standing before her now. There had been times when he demanded sex, but she never refused him. She knew it was part of being a wife. She wondered now what he would have done if she'd refused. Would he have forced her? Was it possible to rape your own wife?

But she was no longer his wife, no longer a pawn in his evil concept of love. She knew now how it felt to be a part of something good—something right (at least for the moment). She knew how it felt to be wanted for just being herself. She knew what it was like to desire a man and be fulfilled.

Candice wiggled and tugged her hands as unobtrusively as possible.

"Our vows said, 'Until *death* do us part.'" He dug the word death into the front of his mouth with his tongue as if metaphorically digging a grave.

"Well if that's how you want it." Her veiled threat was spoken with a velvety tone edged with steel.

"You still think your white knight will show up to rescue you?"

Candice just stared at him refusing to antagonize him any further. She wished she could rub the sting from her face.

"Even if he knows you are at this hotel, he has no idea I'm here or where we are." He smiled. It was exaggerated and forced. "Your rescue mission, I'm afraid, is nonexistent. I'm your knight Baby. I'm here to rescue you from *him*."

Her mouth overruled her mind in its decision to keep quiet. "You can never be the man Landon is." The words spoken so matter-of-factly they could not be refuted.

The kickstand gave way to the expected crash, just like a flickering light giving way to its last sputter of energy before it burns out—Devin's sanity slipped to darkness. He ripped the belt from the loops that held it in place, grabbed the ends together and lurched towards her.

Smack!

Most of the leather hit the chair but a part of it bit into the top of her arm. She winced hard, causing her to pull sharply on the loosening ties on her hand. Her right hand was free! He drew back and brought the belt across her thighs before she could really register the pain in her arm or decide what to do with her free hand. Tears burned hot trails of anger down her brown cheeks. She could tell they were encouraging him and that enraged her.

"You bastard!" She spat out. "You think you can still hurt me? I refuse to let you!"

"Oh yea?" Devin tossed the belt aside, searched for the zipper on his pants and yanked it down. Candice watched what was happening as if it was happening to someone else.

He grabbed her sweater at the center of her chest and jerked her forward, not noticing one hand was free. He slammed his mouth into hers and tried forcing his tongue between her lips. She bit it hard. He yelled out obscenities as she tasted blood on her tongue. Devin held her face roughly with one hand and brought his face near hers again.

"Bite me again Bitch."

Candice spit in his face ridding herself of the foul tang of his blood. Devin slapped her hard across the cheek, stood back and wiped away the moisture from his face. His features cracked into a vulgar smirk and acute terror slammed against Candice's ribcage. He reached for her skirt and violently pulled it down her legs and off of her. He had long since dispensed of her shoes. She guessed it was probably when he knocked her out at the door.

She could not, would not let this happen. He would not violate that part of her. She'd known pleasures that took her passed the horizon. If death is what it took to protect what Landon had given her, then so be it.

Candice kicked wildly. The movements loosened the restraints on her wrist—her other hand was free. When Devin turned to toss her skirt, she quickly rolled over the arm of the chair, landing on the belt. Instinct to grab anything to be used as a weapon forced the belt into her hand. By the time he realized she was free and out of the chair, the expensive belt buckle was coming across his face.

243

Struck into shock, he paused a second too long. Pure adrenaline lifted Candice off of her feet and onto Devin like a tarantula. He was not prepared for the assault and they both landed hard on the floor.

She didn't think they were near anything to knock over, but she thought she'd heard something knocking as they hit the floor. Candice's leg was beneath them and she was sure her ankle was twisted because of the sharp pain that raced up her calf.

Devin's slow reactions from banging his head when they landed were his undoing.

"Haven't you taken enough from me! You sorry Bastard!" The words seemed to rise from the depths of her belly and spew out in sweet release. He did all he could to block the assault her fists whirled on him like a helicopter propeller. She screamed the words over and over with each blow. She didn't know if she was actually hitting him, all she knew was that she couldn't stop fighting back. She was going straight "Tina Turner" on him.

Tears and snot ran down her face as if demons were finally being liberated from her clouded soul. Devin, no longer stunned, recovered from the onslaught and tried to gain the upper hand. He grabbed Candice's wrists and threw his body over, pinning her to the ground, arms above her head.

244

"You're going to have to kill me, Devin Freedman; I promise you that!" Candice forced the words through gritted teeth.

"If it becomes necessary." he replied.

For the first time since the bar, Candice thought about the gun. Devin's hot breath stung her nostrils. He kissed her neck and she remembered instantly her bottom half was exposed. She still had on the tights, but no underwear—vulnerable.

Eyes closed, a strangled scream exploded from her. "Get off of me!" and as if her wish was granted, she felt Devin being lifted away.

"Didn't I tell you to stay away from my wife!"

And there he was at last.

Chapter 25

The Rescue

The security officer who was also a former police detective was poised at the door wearing the housekeeping uniform. The guests on the left and right sides of room 1409 had fortunately checked out early.

The officer knocked. There was a loud thud as if someone had fallen. Landon looked at his dad. They both wore matching frowns standing out of sight range of the peephole. The officer placed one hand on the door handle and the other ready to insert the keycard.

The moment Landon heard Candice scream and curse, his patience was used up. "Open it." His tone was deadly and undisputable. She opened it. Landon pushed through first and the other members of the rescue team followed on his heels. They quickly surveyed the room and spotted Candice pinned beneath Devin on the floor next to the bed.

Landon rushed over and pulled Devin off of Candice all in one motion it seemed. He was immediately torn between beating Devin's ass and seeing if Candice was ok. *How could she be when that maniac was on top of her?* When he freed Candice from her attacker he saw that she was undressed from the waist down.

"What did you do!...What did you do to her!" He almost choked on the words; his rage was so thick.

Devin was lifted to his feet and tossed into the wall. "Didn't I tell you to stay away from my wife?"

Dixon and Colin gave each other a look, but the question went unanswered as they watched Devin flying into another wall without aid of cape or plane. Colin moved forward to intervene, but Dixon stopped him. "This is my son's fight my friend." So Colin just stood back to let Landon have free rein to restructure the hotel room walls.

Landon knew he had to get to Candice. The officer was putting a blanket on her exposed lower half and talking to her. Devin was crumpled on the floor. Landon picked him up and propped him against the wall, holding him there by pressing on the front of his shoulders. "I told you once that if you ever come near my wife, speak to her, look at her, or cause her any kind of discomfort or pain again, when I'm done with you, I promise you're going to be begging for the tortures of hell." Landon punched Devin in his side. "Didn't I tell you that, you bastard?" Devin was too busy trying to grab some oxygen to answer. "How does it feel when someone fights back?"

Though from the looks of his face, Landon thought Candice must have shown him what it felt like.

"Landon." Candice called out to him. She sounded exhausted which further infuriated Landon. "Landon, he's not worth it. I'm ok. It's not as bad as it looks."

Landon looked at the man from foot to head, noticed his pants unzipped and Landon's hand, of its own accord, wrapped tightly around the man's neck. Devin still suspended with Landon's hand acting as a noose.

Dixon was at his side gently touching his arm. "Son, she's right, he's not worth it. He will pay for what he has done. I promise." Landon was breathing heavily as he tore his eyes away from Freedman and looked in his dad's concerned gray eyes. Dixon continued, "She doesn't need to witness anymore violence. She needs you to take care of her."

And with those words, Devin's life was spared.

Landon knew it was against the "man code" to do what he was about to do, but this was no man. "Landon…" she said softly again. He needed to go to her, but first… The movement was swift, hard and completely unexpected by anyone, least of all Devin.

"URGH…ARGH…" Devin slid down the wall again, though this time he would never forget the

248

painful journey. Landon kneed the man so hard in the groin it would take a coal mining search and rescue party to find his balls.

Dixon and Colin both instinctively placed a hand over their manly parts as if to protect them from evil ball-crushing spirits that permeated the air.

She had a swollen lip. How could he have let this happen?

"I'm sorry baby, so sorry. Can you ever forgive me?" He was on his knees with her head in his lap. She hadn't had time to get up. Everything happened so quickly. They'd only been in the room less than a minute but it seemed like a lifetime to Candice. All she wanted was to be in Landon's arms again and have him wipe away the memory of the last couple of hours.

"There is nothing to forgive." She felt him trembling. Or was it her? "You came for me, like I knew you would."

"But I promised you would be safe with me."

"Look at me Landon. I'm safe with you."

Landon did look at her and he didn't like what he saw one bit. He ran his thumb across her swollen bottom lip and rubbed the dried blood from her chin. His jaw was tense as he bit down hard because he felt he would cry. Never had any woman brought him to tears for any reason, but here he was with the most precious creature in the world and someone had harmed her—caused her pain. She was in his care and she'd been abducted, beaten and from the looks of things, nearly raped.

He didn't know it had fallen until he felt Candice wipe away the tear. His worry, fear, frustration and rage from the afternoon were too much to contain. He gathered Candice in his arms and held her tightly there. Tears ran freely and he could not prevent a sob from escaping his lips. Unashamed and thankful he cried for having her back.

Joshua's words came back to him.

It's always the right time Landon.

"I'm never going to let you out of my sight again. Do you hear me?" He said through his tears.

She heard him. What did he mean? *While they were in London? During the trip? Ever?* She would be happy with any option… all of them and she would certainly be happy with staying in his sight forever. But she didn't answer him. She simply said, "I'm ok Landon."

"This is not ok Baby."

No one in the room moved. Dixon and Colin were too stunned to interrupt the scene unfolding before them. It was like Landon was a different person.

He'd always been upbeat and a jokester, but Colin never believed him to be truly happy. There always seemed to be something missing and now he knew his friend had everything he needed. Landon was in love.

"I love you Candice and I will do anything in my power to prevent you from ever being hurt again." He squeezed her tightly again. She winced.

"I'm sorry Baby. Where does it hurt?" He pulled her back a little to look at her better.

"Nowhere. You've healed my heart Landon Phoenix. You love me. You want me. *Me,* Candice Carwin, the girl who is madly in love with *you.* How could anything possibly hurt?"

Epilogue

Loose Ends

Eight months later…

More than thirteen thousand five hundred and five days he'd lived through—thirty-seven years worth. He remembered highlights of some, some small moments of those days he would never forget. Some were a blur and some faded into the shadows of his mind forever. However, Landon knew that if he lived three times as many days, he would never forget the minutest detail of the day he wished he could forget.

He would never forget the sickening terror that seized him when he found out Devin took Candice. He would forever remember her scream of protest. Nor would the image of her struggling beneath him ever leave his mind.

Never would he be able to look at a pair of gray tights on a woman and not see the 2 ½ inch run that was on the knee of *his* woman's tight that day. He would never forget the squeak of the wheel on the gurney that carried Devin away or the two quarters and one dime that had fallen from Candice's purse where Devin dumped the contents on the bed.

His memory would forever hold the surprise of seeing his father, the thankfulness of having him there, the pride of watching him take charge and handle the situation. He would never forget the willingness of his friend to be as discreet as possible. How Jo Ann the female security officer insisted Candice not be questioned at the police station.

Candice refused to go to the hospital as well. She said she just wanted to go home with Landon. So the doctor with the spiky red hair who came to the hotel to check her out examined her in a hotel room. She didn't want to be there either, but it was better than the hospital.

She hated the hospital—hated to see the nurses whispering about her, when they thought she wasn't looking. Or at least that's what she thought they were doing.

The doctor said the bruises would go away after a few days—something she was an expert at knowing. There was a knot on the side of her head that Landon surely would never forget and, like the bruises, never like to see again. She didn't have a concussion but the doctor told Landon to watch her closely for the next couple days.

Landon knew he would never forget the feeling of the tear slipping off of his chin, how it itched a little and then disappeared into Candice's hair. He would never forget how her eyelashes were clumped together from the wetness of her own tears when she told him she was in love with him.

She loved him. Candice shared his feelings. He'd hoped she would but had no idea how profound the news would be to him.

"What are you thinking about?" Candice asked him.

He'd been very quiet on the drive since they left Boston. He always got that way when it was time for her to go back to Baton Rouge.

"I was thinking how happy I am that you love me. How lucky, too."

"I'm the lucky one." She reached over and rubbed her hand along his neck and shoulder.

He leaned his head into the feeling of her touch.

"Yes, you are lucky. I'm a great catch."

Oh how she loved that wicked grin. She pinched him in his ticklish area along his side. The car swerved a little. "Stop woman! You're going to cause an accident." She pretended to do it again.

"Ok...Ok...*I'm* the lucky one." Her smile was intoxicating. Landon continued. "I was also thinking that with the trial and sentencing over, we may be able to finally take that tour of Europe." They'd postponed the trip because neither thought they would enjoy it until they knew Devin was permanently behind bars.

"How can you possibly think about a vacation now with Enrich Corp just getting off of the ground? You still haven't found a buyer for your place in London." She placed her arm on the console that separated them and turned more towards him. "How's that going anyway? Seems like someone would have snatched it up by now, just for the view."

"Well actually how would you feel about keeping it?"

"It's your place Landon. It's up to you if you want to keep it or not." She said it, but would actually be a little sad not to be able to go there anymore.

Landon pulled the car into a rest area and parked.

She frowned and looked at him because they'd only been on the road for about a half an hour.

"Do you have to pee?" She asked.

He laughed a little and turned to her. "No." His tone lost its playful edge and became serious. "When are you going to let me keep you?"

She stared at him, unsure of what he was asking, but hoping it was what she'd been waiting for him to ask—again.

Landon had a fit when she insisted on going back to Baton Rouge after she recovered from her sprained ankle and other bruises. Alex wanted to fly there to be with her but she didn't want to talk about it anymore or watch anyone get that look in their eyes when they were feeling sorry for her. Landon had accused her of running away from them but she had to do what was best for her at the time and she wanted to go back to what was familiar for a while.

Landon *insisted* that they should marry immediately because he didn't want to be without her. Candice refused. She wanted to be completely free of Devin first. She wanted to wait until the trial and sentencing was done. When she became Candice Phoenix, she didn't want to ever have to see or hear about Devin again.

Now the trial and sentencing was over. It was finally over. Devin was sentenced to 32 years in prison for kidnapping, aggravated assault, stalking and attempted rape. They never connected anyone from British Airways to Devin for leaking the address where the luggage was being sent.

Landon was swamped with getting his business started. He and Ethan had an excellent team, but it was quite time consuming, much different from the life he had as a pilot. He spent most of his time in Boston. She and Landon saw each other often but like him, she longed to not have to leave him every weekend.

It was Saturday so that meant she was supposed to leave the next day. They were meeting Joshua and Alex in Concord for a fundraiser they were sponsoring. It was a Jazz concert to raise money for programs for the arts for inner city kids. The drive was nice. She really enjoyed the fall foliage.

Candice watched a little girl pick up a diaper her mom dropped while juggling a baby and all the things that went with it. She wondered what a baby with Landon would look like—a perfect blend of her chocolate skin and his creamy tone. She wondered what color eyes he or she would have.

"Candice…"

She turned to him again.

"If you aren't ready yet I understand." Though he was really disappointed that she would not commit to him officially.

"I'm ready."

His brilliant blue-gray eyes seemed to register what she said before his mind did. She could have sworn they shot off a spark.

"You're ready?" He blinked, hoping for a positive response and that he'd heard her correctly.

"Yes Landon, I'm ready." She smiled and watched him quickly unbuckle the seatbelt, get out of the car and run over to her side. He jerked the handle on the door.

"Ouch!" Landon shook his fingers then put the side of his thumb in his mouth. "Damit!" He knocked on the window looking at a grinning Candice.

"Unlock the door woman." She did. He opened it successfully this time. "You're laughing at me?"

She clamped her mouth shut and shook her head "no."

"Yes you are. Come here." He reached in, unsnapped the belt, reached for her hand and pulled her out. "I'll show you what happens when you laugh at me."

Hands on her hips and head cocked to the side, she said, "What ha—"

He stole the rest of the word right off of her lips with his, removed it completely with a swipe of his tongue. Her laughter turned into a moan as he greedily searched out her tongue. A car horn reminded them they were in public. He broke the kiss and placed his forehead on hers.

"We will finish that later." he said.

Excitement and anticipation settled between her thighs as she mentally counted the hours until "later" would come.

"Are you saying you will finally marry me, Candice Carwin?"

"Yes Landon, that's what I'm saying."

Landon pulled her to his chest and held her tightly as he was accustomed to doing with her. "I love you so much, Candice. Right now I would love nothing better than to make love to my future wife." He stroked her cheek with the back of his hand. "You would wait until we were on the interstate, away from a bed, to finally agree. I don't want you to leave me tomorrow. It breaks my heart every time I have to watch you go."

"Ok." The word was simple yet full of promise.

"Ok?" He pushed away from her, cocked his head and asked again. "Ok? You mean you don't have to go back tomorrow."

"Nope." She smiled up at him loving her little surprise. She had no intentions to go back. Her place was with Landon. She was ready. She already had her things packed and ready to move across the country, though she wasn't bringing much—just her clothes and art supplies.

"Oh, Baby." He hugged her again and held her there until a bee buzzed by and she sneezed. "Come on let's get you in the car. Did you take your allergy meds today?"

She got back in the car and he reached in.

"I can snap my own seat Landon." He smiled and kissed her. "I wasn't reaching in for that." He fished something out of the center console. "I was reaching in for this." Landon presented her with a small gray velvety box. The hinges squeaked when she opened it. She giggled and looked up at him. "Sounds like a coffin closing in an old scary movie."

"Woman! I'm trying to be romantic here."

She put her fingers over her lips and pretended to appear serious.

He squatted in the opened car door because kneeling would have gotten his suit dirty. "Let's just say we are laying your old life to rest. It is gone. All of the bad stuff is dead to us."

She gasped. The ring was beautiful. It looked vintage and classy. It was so her. He pulled the ring out of the box and slid it on her trembling finger. "This ring is a promise to you that your life will be full of happiness and wonderful adventures by my side. I can't wait to share my life with you, my everything."

"Oh Landon." Before she could stop it or turn away, "Achoo!" He wiped his face.

"Thanks for sharing. You got this whole romance thing down don't you?"

"If nothing else, it makes a great story." She quickly grabbed a tissue from her purse and wiped his face. "Sorry Babe."

"I love you my quirky beautiful woman." He stood and kissed her and walked to his side of the car. Neither could stop smiling. She looked down at her hand, back at him and they both laughed out loud.

"I'll arrange for a company to pack and move your things immediately." He said as he pulled back on to the interstate.

"Not necessary. Already done."

Landon turned to look at Candice. His smile broadened but he didn't say anything more as he focused back on the road.

They rode in silence for a while. Candice wished she had time to stop and paint the brilliant colors, then remembered she could make the time in the next week or so since she would be staying with

Landon. Staying with Landon. She reached over and squeezed his arm. He smiled at her.

"Yes, I'm happy too."

Candice turned a little in her seat so she could look at Landon. Damn he was so good looking. And he's all mine she thought. *Every night with Landon Phoenix. Every morning with Landon Phoenix. My Landon.* She tried not to squeeze her thighs together but couldn't help the reflex. It was best to just change the subject.

"Will your mom and dad be at the concert? And by the way, do we have to tell her we are getting married."

The *her* she was referring to was most definitely his mom. Landon laughed. He remembered all the hell his mother put Alex through when they announced their engagement and she was most likely remembering it too.

"I doubt if my mom is going. It's not really her thing and as far as your other question goes, yes we do. I want to tell the world, but we will get married on our own terms."

She smiled. "Good. When?"

Landon pretended to steer the car towards an upcoming exit. "We can go right now if you want."

262

She laughed. "I wouldn't mind, but I really would like my parents there and Alex."

He steered back on the path. "Ok. I really would like my father and brother there as well."

"I'm so glad you have made peace with your father. I really like him."

"He's crazy about you. I need to be careful or he may try to take you from me."

She smiled again thinking of the kindness he showed to her in London and all the times she'd seen him since. "Oh yea, we have got to invite Colin."

"Well you plan it baby and they will come."

Candice looked around at all the people who had come out to support programs for the arts for kids. The concert was a sit-down dinner with a dance floor and live musicians. The entire ballroom was decorated with art from students in the surrounding areas. Some students were set to perform with famous musicians like Wynton Marsalis and the Vijay Iyer Trio. Landon's friend Sophia had a group of kids who were going to demonstrate some Latin dances.

Candice thought Joshua and Alex did a wonderful job organizing the benefit. Everyone was thrilled not only with the turnout, but with the news of Candice and Landon's engagement. Dixon gave them both a big warm fatherly hug and wished them well. He promised to keep Jocelyn off of their backs during the planning, which wouldn't be too difficult. She was spending a lot of time in New York lately, for what; he didn't really care enough to concern himself with finding out.

Landon noticed his father was alone again. He hadn't seen his mother in quite some time. She was either at some club meeting or out of town for a charity event that helped no one who actually needed it.

Needless to say, she was not thrilled to find out he and Candice were a hot item when he returned to Boston. The first time he brought Candice over after he'd moved back to Boston, his mother was overtly rude and refused to even acknowledge her as Landon's girlfriend.

It was a small dinner party with some of his parent's old friends and their single or divorced daughters—so typical of his mother. The first time she introduced Landon to a woman as if Candice wasn't standing there he ignored it, but to his surprise his father didn't. He'd asked his mother to speak to him privately. When they returned, his mother had a perfect smiled plastered on her perfect face, but he could tell she was livid. When it was time to sit for dinner, Landon noticed he wasn't seated next to Candice.

Candice assured him it was ok, but when his mother openly suggested he escort Penny what's-her-name to some gala, he rose excused himself from the table, walked around to Candice and told her they were leaving.

Dixon was mortified at his wife's behavior and again wondered why he'd put up with it for so many years. It was the first time Landon saw his father stand up to his mother, but from his behavior over the recent weeks he'd been back, it wasn't the first time.

"Jocelyn, you owe Candice an apology. Your behavior is childish and asinine."

Too shocked to speak, she simply stared at Dixon.

"I said, you owe Candice an apology."

"You have got to be kidding, Dixon." She picked up her fork and knife and continued to cut her chicken breast.

Dixon stood. "I'm sorry, but the party is over. Thank you for coming, but my wife's behavior prevents us from going any further in the evening. Have a good night and drive safely." At first everyone thought he was just kidding, but when he asked the caterers to clear the table, they knew it was no joke. Landon looked at his mom—her features like stone. She made no eye contact with anyone. Dixon walked over to Landon and Candice as the guest filed out in disbelief of the unprecedented events and suggested they go to Alex's sports bar. They did, leaving Jocelyn sitting at the table with the caterers. Landon looked back, sadden for his mother. Her life was shallow and empty.

"Babe, are you ok?" Candice asked him.

"Yes, just worried about my dad. He seems really distracted tonight." Landon watched his father for a moment. He was staring at the entrance. He saw his father smile and physically relax. Turning to the entrance, he saw Gloria his dad's secretary, walk in and search the crowd as if she was looking for her party—his dad, no doubt.

Landon wasn't sure how he felt about watching his father get excited when another woman besides his mom walked in the door. As a matter of fact, he'd never seen his father get excited to see his mom. Maybe he would try to bring the subject of Gloria up when he met with his father later in the week.

He was learning a lot from his dad since he'd given him Global Green. He and Ethan didn't have to pay a dime for the company nor did they need investors. When Dixon found out Landon was one of the buyers of the company he acquired in a takeover, he gave it to him under the condition that Landon hold controlling interest in the company. Ethan didn't like it at first but felt that it was beneficial in the long run to begin a company in the black.

The two men worked well together. He, Ethan and Joshua had gone out sailing and fishing several times and were becoming fast friends. They also found they had a lot in common.

"Landon, isn't this a great turnout?" Alex hugged him excitedly.

"Yes, Alex it is. Hopefully we can raise enough money to make a difference."

"I believe so, but of course the arts programs can always use more. I'm thankful Sophia got some of her clients involved for free!"

Landon smiled and looked out on the dance floor. "She's great isn't she?"

"Yep, but I'm surprised she's not married."

"Ha! Sophia? Married? Never!"

"Remember Phoenix, we used to say those same words about you."

"Touché my beautiful sister-in-law." He loved Alex. She was perfect for Joshua. He didn't think she stood a whole five feet tall, but her attitude and spunk stood her at least seven feet in the air. Her pretty caramel face with those huge dimples suckered many a

267

helpless victim to whatever cause she was championing at the moment.

"Plus I've been seeing she and Ethan checking each other out when they think no one is looking."

Landon looked where Alex was looking and just as she said, Ethan was watching Sophia as she danced with Joshua. Candice walked up to him and he looked away to talk to her. When he looked back towards the dance floor Sophia was gone. Landon watched Ethan search her out until he spotted her again.

Maybe Alex was on to something.

Ethan Powers was sure it was the same woman from that awful day a year ago. She either didn't remember him or was pretending not to, but he was sure it was her. She'd been pretty distraught that day so it was possible she didn't remember or had blocked the memory from her mind.

He, however, had not been able to get her out of his head. He had held her and she fit so well in his arms. Ethan didn't know how many nights he'd awaken from dreaming about her. She haunted him, but apparently she was good friends with Landon and the whole lot of *them*. How unfortunate.

When he's done with them the Phoenix name will be worthless. He was determined to get back everything that was taken from him.

A malicious smile darkened his face as he lifted the glass of wine to his lips. He downed the liquid, placed it on a table nearby, took one last look at Sophia, sighed heavily with regret and walked towards the exit.

Dear Reader,

I had a ball writing *Surrendered Pleasures*. Candice and Landon became a part of my life as I hope they have become a part of yours. There are so many drafts of this book that I have lost count. I tried to steer these characters in the directions I wanted them to go, but they had other plans. Instead, they whispered their story to me and I was simply the recorder of it. I hope you enjoyed their surrender as much as I did.

You, of course, have not seen the last of the Phoenix men and their wives. Look forward to catching up with them in the third and final (as of now, but who knows) novel in the **Pleasures Collection**.

Also the mystery surrounding Ethan Powers will be revealed as he tries desperately to avoid and forget the beautiful and sassy Sophia Ilarraza. Expect the unexpected in my next novel, *Seductive Pleasures*.

Sincerely,
Natasha Simmons

www.ingramcontent.com/pod-product-compliance
Lightning Source LLC
Chambersburg PA
CBHW061559170626
46811CB00001B/252

* 9 7 8 0 9 8 8 2 9 9 4 0 5 *